the Beginning

the
Beginning

A prequel to Karen Kingsbury's
The Bridge

KAREN KINGSBURY

HOWARD BOOKS
A DIVISION OF SIMON & SCHUSTER, INC.

New York   Nashville   London   Toronto   Sydney   New Delhi

Howard Books
A Division of Simon & Schuster, Inc.
1230 Avenue of the Americas
New York, NY 10020

ISBN: 978-1-4767-1355-7

CHAPTER ONE

Fall 1971

The pains began at two-thirty in the morning.

A sharp, twisting sort of pain that woke up Donna Barton and sent panic coursing through her veins.

"Charlie!" She screamed his name, and immediately he sat up in bed beside her.

"What?" He was breathless, frantic. Ready to carry her to safety or tackle monsters on her behalf. For a few seconds he looked from one side of the room to the other getting his bearings. Then he seemed to remember. His eyes met hers. "The baby!" Even in the dim moonlight it was easy to see the color leave his face. "Is it time?"

Donna closed her eyes. The pain moved in waves

down her stomach, across her lower spine. She tightened her legs, fighting it. "I'm . . . not sure."

"It must be." He threw off the covers and ran across the room to a small heap on the floor. Yesterday's clothes. He pulled on the pair of shorts and T-shirt.

Sweat beaded on her forehead. *Hurry, Charlie. Hurry.* This was the hottest North Carolina fall in fifty-two years. The heat and humidity made her feel like she was underwater.

He ran to her, his eyes wide. "Your bag's ready. Stay here. I'll get your clothes."

Something cool. She needed something cool. "Maybe my—" Her pain doubled. "Charlie!" Fear mixed with desperation. Each word came slowly. "What if . . . what if it's too . . . strong?"

"It's not . . . it's normal." His voice was higher than before, strained and breathy. Like he was trying to convince himself. "We have to get you to the hospital."

The pain didn't fade like Donna expected a contraction might do.

Normal.

Yes, that was what she was feeling. This pain was good and right and normal. Pains that would bring their baby into the world and make them a family. A beautiful pain that would erase all the pain she'd already lived through. They needed to go. She would wear her nightgown. She slid her feet onto the floor, but her lungs refused to work. "Help . . . me!"

"Baby, don't move!" Charlie was at her side, her bag flung over his shoulder. "I'll carry you."

Donna felt her body go limp as he scooped her into his arms. Her breaths came in short, shallow gasps. "I'm . . . scared."

"Hold on . . . I'll get you there."

She couldn't keep her eyes open. Somewhere in the back alleys of her mind she felt herself moving, felt him carrying her. But the pain became a thick, dark, suffocating lava, pulling her in, covering her, consuming her. His voice was only a faint whisper now, and finally she couldn't fight the pull another minute.

In the blackness that overcame her, she reminded herself once more of the truth. This was a good pain. Her past swirled before her, the terrible sad reality alive again. Before the chapter when she met Charlie Barton, Donna's story was dark and depressing, one pathetic page after another. The only child of a couple of drug addicts, Donna never stood a chance. Other boys and girls went home to hugs and help with homework.

Not Donna.

She would walk through the front door to her parents crashed on the floor or keeled over on the dirty sofa. Drugs sat in the open, plastic bags of white powder and dark green crushed leaves. Needles and mirrors and razor blades and matches. It was the sixties, but even so, Donna's parents were ahead of the drug game.

Donna wanted nothing to do with their world so she found one of her own. The world of books. She earned straight As and didn't come home from school until she absolutely had to. None of her teachers was surprised when Donna earned valedictorian honors or when she received a full-ride scholarship to North Carolina State. Donna was tempted to believe that the sad parts of her story were behind her.

She was wrong. Her mom overdosed on heroin three days before her graduation.

Donna's English teacher took her in until she headed off for North Carolina, but left alone, her father didn't handle the loss well. A month later he went out one night with his friends and never came home. Police found his car wrapped around a tree the next morning. And like that, Donna was alone in the world.

That was real pain. The pain that lived within for years after, one that came back without warning, taking her breath away with its severity.

This . . . this aching, stabbing, tightening . . . this was life. A variation of the sort of happy reds and vibrant oranges and brilliant blues that had colored her existence since God led her to Charlie Barton. She let herself focus on the beginning, the first day she saw Charlie. Within minutes of meeting him he made her do something as foreign as it was fantastic.

He made her laugh.

Charlie was the only son of a local cement contractor, but despite his father's mandate, he had no intention of pouring cement for a living. Charlie was innovative and sensitive. When he earned his degree in business it created a rift between him and his father that still remained. The broken relationship reminded Charlie of a thousand times growing up when his father would discourage his academics and the craziest thing of all.

His dad forbade him to read.

The rule only made Charlie more determined. He'd sneak books into his backpack from the school library and read them under the covers by flashlight late at night. Books opened a new world to Charlie, a world of *Tom Sawyer* and *Robinson Crusoe* and *Treasure Island*.

But books remained a secret for Charlie. Only after he and Donna had been dating for several months did he tell her about his private love for stories, and his greatest dream of all.

The dream of opening a bookstore.

Her memories mixed together in the darkness. Just last week Charlie had called his father, looking to make amends. Instead the man had lit into him, berating him and reminding him that he would never amount to anything. That he was a failure. *You're a Barton, and*

Bartons aren't businesspeople. You'll fail, and then you'll come crawling back to me and the cement.

A knife couldn't have left deeper scars.

Donna's pain grew stronger, twisting her insides and burning through her body. She needed to get to the hospital. Giving birth shouldn't feel like this, right? Maybe she was dying. She wasn't sure. Her thoughts were less clear now, less organized. They swirled and faded and grew more distant until only two things remained.

Her pain and the darkness.

CHAPTER TWO

The bad feeling plagued Edna Carlton from the moment she got out of bed.

She opened her eyes, stretched her legs to the empty side of the mattress, and like a sudden storm, it hit her. A sense of doom, or despair. Darker than despair. Outside her bedroom window a pair of bluebirds swapped familiar songs, and the smell of sweet jasmine wafted on a cool breeze through the screen. The day looked perfect, beautiful. Everything in all of life was fine.

So why did she suddenly feel like the world was ending?

Edna climbed out of bed and walked to the kitchen. Coffee. That's what she needed . . . fresh coffee. She added water to the kettle and turned on the flame beneath it.

The jar of instant Maxwell House sat nearby. A couple of spoonfuls of the dark granules in the bottom of her grandmother's china teacup and she was ready to go.

She stared out the back window of her small apartment. The only thing louder than the silence was her fear, closing in on her, reminding her that she was alone. Tom didn't have a break until Christmas—if then. For a long moment she closed her eyes and tried to remember the last time she'd gotten a letter from him. A week at least, longer than usual.

Maybe that explained the ominous feeling. Letters were the only reminder that he was still alive, still fighting battles in Vietnam, still doing what he felt called to do as an American citizen. Tom . . . the love of her life.

The Bible talked about two becoming one, and their friends used to tease how that was never truer than for Edna and Tom. They were right. Sometimes Edna couldn't figure out where Tom ended and she began. They were that close, that inseparable.

Before he went to war, anyway.

The kettle rattled and a low whistle began. She flipped off the flame and poured water into the cup. Beneath her feet the linoleum was cold, typical for late fall in Franklin, Tennessee. But this morning it spread a chill up her body and into her bones. Her teeth chattered as she brought the hot cup to her face and breathed in.

What was this oppressive feeling? Why today? She

held onto the cup with both hands, letting the heat work its way through her. The calendar on the wall seemed to taunt her, reminding her how long six months really was. Six frightening, painful, lonely months. She studied October's little boxes, stared at the place where the square white pages hung near the refrigerator. If only she could look ahead and know the future. Peek in on the time when Tom would be home and they could truly begin their life together.

They'd only been married three weeks when he shipped out.

She sipped her coffee and let herself go back to the beginning. The way she often did when she missed him. Through grade school, Tom had been the one person Edna couldn't tolerate. Every recess he would run by and tug on her blond ponytail or tease her for being too slow or too smart or any of a dozen reasons. She did everything she could to fly under his radar.

The summer before middle school, Edna begged her mother to enroll her in a different district so she wouldn't have to spend the next three years taking classes with Tom Carlton. Her mother only rolled her eyes and told her what she always told her.

"That boy has a crush on you, Edna. I keep telling you."

Edna wanted to wear a disguise the first day of classes, but instead she connected with a group of her girlfriends and hoped for safety in numbers. The plan worked the first week, but the next Monday Tom came up behind her and flicked her hair.

"Hey . . . haven't seen you."

Edna turned and felt her cheeks grow hot. "I . . . I've been busy."

"Oh." He grinned at her. "Well . . . in case I don't see you around, you should probably know."

Confusion added to her nervousness. "Know what?"

He started to run off, but as he did he winked at her. "You're the prettiest girl in sixth grade."

She literally stopped in place, suddenly not sure which class she was heading to, which way was up. It had never occurred to her after all these years that her mother might be right. After that, she still did her best to avoid Tom Carlton. But by the end of the year she was no longer afraid of him, and in seventh grade they had become friends.

Tom liked to say it took him most of his life to get up the courage to ask her out, but when their freshman year in high school came and the football team had its annual bonfire, he sat beside her. After two hours of small talk he did what he'd wanted to do as far back as he could remember.

He asked her out.

They were inseparable after that, the sort of couple people smiled at when they walked past. Their senior year they were voted homecoming king and queen, and after the dance Tom asked her to marry him. Their future looked brighter than the lights on Broadway in downtown Nashville. Only one thing threatened to dim them.

The draft.

Tom turned nineteen the summer after high school, and a month later he was drafted to join the army offensive in Vietnam. While many of their friends enrolled in college, became conscientious objectors, or feigned injuries and illnesses to avoid serving the United States, Tom wouldn't hear of it.

"If I'm asked to serve, I'll serve." His smile was tinged with sadness. "We'll get married before I go." He pulled her close and kissed her. "I'll get my years of serving out of the way. Then we'll start real life."

Six more months and he'd be finished with his tour, done with fighting. Six months. Another sip of coffee. Just a bad dream, that's all. Her husband was fighting half a world away. Of course she'd have bad dreams now and then. She tried to keep her fingers from shaking. But if it was only a bad dream, why wasn't the awful feeling gone? Instead, the feeling suffocated her, its tenacious claws set deep.

Half a cup of coffee in slow, nervous sips, and finally she made a plan. She would clean the apartment. Not the usual washing down the kitchen and folding laundry, but deep cleaning. The baseboards along the hallway and the dust on the top rims of the photo frames. A cleaning that would take her all day, and by the time sunset came she would've worked the bad feeling out of her system.

Edna grabbed a spray bottle and a rag and headed for the bathroom. She was on her hands and knees washing the floor at the base of the toilet when she heard the doorbell.

The smell of Pine-Sol, the feel of the wet rag in her hands, the pinch of tiled floor against her knees, all of it froze into a single instant, a moment she absolutely knew she would remember forever. *Don't get up, Edna . . . Don't do it.* Don't answer the door. She closed her eyes but the doorbell rang again, and she couldn't stop herself. Couldn't keep from scrambling to her feet and hurrying blindly to the front of the apartment.

She didn't check the peephole, didn't stop to see who was on the other side. She already knew. This was the reason for the feeling, the doom that had smothered her since she opened her eyes that morning. *Not Tom, God . . . please . . . not Tom.* He only has six more months . . .

Her rebel hand defied her heart and suddenly the door was open, and there they were. Two sad-eyed, fresh-faced soldiers in sharply pressed uniforms. One of them had a telegram.

"No!" she shouted. Spots danced in front of her eyes

and they quickly began to connect. She couldn't breathe or move or remember where she was. "Not Tom!"

They were the last words she remembered saying. She began to fall, but she didn't care. The floor could take her life and that would be a relief compared to living in a world without her Tom. One final thought screamed at her before she passed out. The date. October 5, 1971. A date that would stand forever as a dividing line in time.

Life before the doorbell rang, and life after.

CHAPTER THREE

⎯⎯⎯⎯⎯⎯⎯⎯⎯⎯

The baby was a girl.

That's what they told Donna when she woke up. Charlie was at her side, tears streaming down his cheeks. He pressed his face close to hers. "You're alive . . . I can't believe you're alive."

She felt weak and thin. Too thin. "What . . . what happened?"

Charlie eased back, his eyes wide. For the first time since she'd known him, the confident sparkle in his eyes was gone. In its place was a fear that made him look like a different man altogether. "You almost died."

"The baby, Charlie. What happened to our baby?"

His silence told her more than his words ever could. He swallowed and let his eyes find a spot on the floor. For a long time he only shook his head, as if the details were too awful to speak. But eventually the story came. In tragic bits and terrible pieces, it came.

The contractions were too strong; Donna had been right. Something had gone wrong on the inside, and she had started bleeding—so much that her body had gone into shock and the bleeding became profuse. Every organ, every cell, bleeding out. D-I-C, Charlie called it. He couldn't remember what it stood for. Or why it happened.

"It took . . . everyone in the emergency room, Donna. No one thought you were going to—"

He couldn't say the words. Donna's heartbeat slammed around in her chest. "The baby, Charlie . . . tell me."

Again he shook his head. "She . . . she didn't make it." He looked through her, to the places in her soul where only he was allowed. "They couldn't save her."

Donna squeezed her eyes shut. She couldn't acknowledge her daughter's death without first acknowledging the most beautiful part of the story. They'd had a daughter. He was saying something about her blood loss, but Donna couldn't make out the words. Her question cut him off midsentence. "Charlie . . . What did she look like?"

Charlie stopped talking.

Her eyes flew open. "Please, Charlie. Tell me what she looked like."

A series of sobs shook him and he hung his head, his hands over his face. After a minute he found his voice. "She was perfect . . . I only saw her for a minute. She . . . she looked just like you, Donna."

Her baby girl looked like her! Where was she, then? Where was her baby now? How dare someone take her away without letting Donna hold her first? She wanted to ask, wanted to know what cruel doctor had taken her daughter's body without her permission. But the questions pummeled her heart and left her exhausted. Too defeated to speak.

Charlie stroked her damp hair and brought his face close to hers again. "We'll get through this . . . we will."

Before Donna could consider the possibility, the doctor walked into the room. His expression didn't look much better than Charlie's. "Mrs. Barton . . . I'm so sorry."

With all her remaining energy she opened the palm of her hand and stretched out her fingers. Charlie covered her hand with his own, wrapping her fingers with his, skin to skin. The doctor was saying something about their baby's body being disposed of at the morgue.

"What . . . what about a funeral?"

The doctor blinked, his mouth slightly open. "That . . . that isn't how we do things. Your baby was born dead, Mrs. Barton."

"She deserves a funeral."

Only then did Donna realize she hadn't cried yet. Her eyes were dry, paralyzed with the news. But at the realization that her daughter was already gone, that there would be no baby to hold, no body to bury, sobs gathered in her chest and a river of sadness began flowing from her eyes.

"Thank you, Doctor," Charlie held her hand more tightly, "for saving Donna's life."

Her husband's relief touched her, but it didn't ease the pain. And then, as if there were room inside her for more heartache, the doctor delivered the final blow. "We had to remove your uterus, Mrs. Barton." He looked like he'd rather stop practicing medicine than say this next part. "You won't be able to have more children. I'm . . . so sorry."

Donna didn't hear what came after that. She closed her eyes and turned toward Charlie, only Charlie. Their daughter was dead, and there would be no babies, not ever. No children running through their home, no sweet laughter, no trips to the park. Just her and Charlie and the empty days that lay ahead.

Time wouldn't stop for her heartbreak. Somehow, without her approval, the days marched on, a series of unforgiving sunrises fading into a blur of sunsets. From her first day back in their North Carolina townhouse, Donna knew one thing for certain: If Charlie was right, if they were going to be okay, then they needed a reason to live. Charlie's father had learned of the tragedy and he'd reached out, called Charlie to come home, back to the cement business. But Charlie politely declined. His father called him a fool, and the rift was back.

Alone again, just them and God against the world, they took long walks while Donna tried to regain her strength. Eventually they came up with a plan. Their own pain would grow dim if only they could find a way to help other people. What they needed was something to pour all their energy and love, their passion and longing, into. Something that would take the place of the family they'd never have. It took six weeks before the idea hit them. By then they had searched the map for a new home, a new beginning, and every search led them to the same place.

Franklin, Tennessee.

Franklin with its small-town feel just twenty minutes south of Nashville's Music Row. Main Street was expanding. A mercantile, a theater, a bank, and three cafés. They could live a few blocks away and figure out how to help, a way to be part of the foundation of a town on the rise.

If only they could help people who were hurting. She and Charlie could pour into their lives, listen to their stories, and point them in the right direction. If they could be a part of changing the lives of others, then their own pain was sure to grow dim.

They would find a church once they arrived in town, but that wasn't where their helping would happen. Not at an orphanage or a homeless shelter. They didn't feel God calling them to either of those places. Their help would happen somewhere else, at the most likely place of all. At a place she and Charlie could believe in.

A bookstore.

A small-town bookstore would bridge the pain of yesterday to the promise of tomorrow. By the end of the year they found just the building, a small two-story house on Franklin's Main Street, a place that had long ago housed Civil War soldiers. It was made of brick and old pine, and it smelled faintly like Lemon Pledge and campfire smoke, a smell that welcomed them from the first time they toured it. They were approved for a business loan, and like that, the catharsis began. With every painted wall and built-in bookshelf, Donna could feel God healing them, sense Him smiling down.

Because the bookstore would absolutely change lives.

No question, somewhere, someone else needed a bridge in his or her own life, a way to find hope for the future. Because of that, when it came time to open their doors, the bookstore's name was already decided.

They called it The Bridge.

CHAPTER FOUR

The days blended one into the other. One month after another.

Some days Edna didn't get out of bed. She would lay on her side, her knees curled up to her waist, holding tight to one of Tom's T-shirts, clinging to it, cradling the soft worn cotton to her chest. Her parents had moved up north to New Hampshire after Edna's high school graduation. They were crushed by the news that Tom had been killed in action. The next day they flew down and stayed for Tom's funeral. But after a week they had to return to their lives.

Edna understood.

"Spend time with friends, dear. That's all you can do." Her mom looked stricken as she kissed her cheek on the way out. "You could always move up north with us."

But that was never really an option. She and Tom had picked out this apartment together and they had lived here, husband and wife, for three weeks. Three whole weeks of laughter and bliss and happily ever after. Their entire married life. Tom liked the view of the park from the window and the way it was only a couple of blocks' walk to Main Street and downtown Franklin. She could still see him sitting at the kitchen table.

If Edna moved now, she would lose all that remained of him.

Her mom was right about her friends. They were there and they were willing. The problem was hers. Most of the time she didn't answer the door when they came to call, too busy staring into space and trying to remember how to walk without falling to the floor in pain.

Her heart was that broken.

After a few months, her friends came less often. When Edna would invite one of them in for a cup of coffee, the conversation was always awkward. They would forever feel sorry for her, and she would forever be the victim. When the New Year rolled around, Edna was still talking to Tom's photograph before she fell asleep. Still terrified about tomorrow. Still waking up each morning to the truth about Tom's death hitting her all over again.

But she was running out of money. That was the

only reason she had to finally get dressed and leave the apartment. The stipend given her by the army for Tom's death while on active duty was running out. Still the process of leaving the house was slow. Day after day she tried and failed.

She had no idea where to work or what she would do. She had no skills to speak of, no training. Before Tom's death she watched two neighbor kids to supplement Tom's military income. Babysitting was out of the question now. She couldn't focus long enough to remember what day it was, let alone take on the responsibility of watching children. Especially when she and Tom would never have any of their own. Lying in her bed she only knew that she wanted to work somewhere on Main Street—Tom's favorite place.

It took four painful days to go from forming a plan to actually stepping through the front door and walking to Main Street. But on that fourth day Edna actually did it. She got dressed, did her hair, and walked to Main Street. The café wasn't hiring, and neither was Cal's Drugstore. But at the mercantile, Edna met the manager near the front counter. The woman was kind with gray hair and bright eyes.

"Hello." She held out her hand. "I'm Edna Carlton. I . . . need a job. If you're hiring, that is." Her words sounded forced and awkward. She stepped back, her knees shaking.

"Hmm." She studied Edna for a quick moment. "I *am* looking for someone to ring sales in the afternoons. I'm supposed to be retired." She smiled sweetly. "Minimum wage, but room for advancement."

Edna wasn't sure what to say, but she knew one thing—she had to be honest. "I . . . don't know how to ring sales."

"Oh, dear, I can train you on that. I'm looking for friendly and teachable. And I have a hunch you're all of that."

"Yes, ma'am." Edna stood a little straighter. "Can I fill out an application?"

"Tell you what." She pointed to the back of the store where the soda fountain always drew a crowd. "Let's sit and have a milkshake. Half an hour from now I'll have what I need to know."

Edna smiled, a feeling she'd almost forgotten. An hour later she had an apron and a job. When she stepped outside onto Main Street and started north toward her apartment she realized something.

She had only thought about Tom a few times in the last hour. That, and she was walking and breathing and taking on responsibility like a regular person. It was the first time she had even the slightest glimmer of hope that she might survive. Even so she cried herself to sleep, desperate to tell Tom about her new job and the way she was trying to meet life head-on.

Not until she'd been working for a week did she notice the bookstore.

It looked quaint and cute, a storefront with a brand-new sign, just a few doors down from the mercantile. She came closer and read the wording in the window. Disappointment settled over her. It had closed ten minutes earlier, but as she stood outside the place, gradually a thought came to light in Edna's soul.

She had forgotten about books.

Maybe that was the answer. She might not have much of a life of her own, but every book would be another escape, a way to live without actually having to do anything more than read.

Edna stared at the place, at the warm light in the windows, and she made up her mind. Tomorrow before work she would visit the bookstore. She had a feeling she would like being inside. The shelves were full, and in the back of the place she could see a worn leather sofa and a chair near a fireplace. She even liked the name.

The Bridge.

As she walked home she realized she had reached another benchmark, another signpost on her journey to living again. She was no longer afraid of tomorrow.

At least in this moment, she was actually looking forward to it.

CHAPTER FIVE

The grand opening of The Bridge happened the first weekend of January 1972. In some ways, Donna couldn't believe how quickly God had given them their dream. The craziness of moving to Franklin and getting the business loan, buying the building and redoing the inside so it would be the cozy, welcoming bookstore they wanted it to be. All of it seemed to happen in a blur.

A blur that kept Donna from missing her baby girl in all but the latest hours of the night. Hours when she should've been feeding her or rocking her or singing her quiet songs about Jesus. Cradling her close in a pink blanket.

Charlie was so happy about The Bridge, he almost never talked about the heartache they left behind in

North Carolina. He never cried late at night the way she did, at least she never heard him. Donna kept her tears to herself. They were getting on, moving ahead with life. If the tears came at night, so be it. She would probably always cry when she thought about their baby girl.

But in the daytime, their new life as bookstore owners was too exciting to do anything but celebrate. They stocked the shelves with every sort of fiction and nonfiction title. There were books about war and books about peace, volumes on making a casserole and tales of historical fiction. American favorites, British classics, and contemporary fiction.

Donna's favorite part of the bookstore was the front room with the sofa and chair they'd purchased for around the fireplace. The welcome feeling was immediate as soon as a customer walked through the door. *Come in. Sit a while. Take your time.* Words Donna and Charlie told their customers from the first day.

The Bridge had been opened a few weeks when a pretty blond woman walked through the door at noon one day. She was young, in her early twenties at the most. But there was something old about her eyes.

"Hello." Donna smiled at her.

"Hi." The woman looked away, at the titles that hung over the nearest set of shelves. "I'm just looking."

"Okay." Donna settled back in her seat behind the

counter. "Take your time." *This one looks like she's hurting, Lord.* Was she sick or suffering from a broken heart? Did she live alone in the area without family? Donna caught a glimpse of the woman's wedding ring. She kept her questions to herself. Some people who walked through the door needed a little time to find their way.

Charlie walked up and put his arm around Donna. "We're out of *Little Women.*" He kissed her on the cheek. "Four copies out the door in the last two days!"

The blond woman worked her way farther from the checkout counter, down another aisle, and out of sight. Donna held her finger to her lips. "She's sad. Not sure why."

"Who?" Charlie dropped his voice to barely a whisper. He peered down the closest aisle and pointed, his eyes questioning. "That way?"

"Yes. A young woman." Compassion stirred Donna. "A little younger than us. Something's wrong. I can tell."

"Okay." He nodded, his eyes bright. "I'll pray." In the purchase order book by the register, Charlie jotted down a note to buy more copies of *Little Women.* Then he returned to his inventory at the back of the store.

After a few minutes the young woman made her way back to the cash register. She folded her arms, and Donna could see that her hands were shaking. "I . . . need something to read."

"Okay." Donna faced her so only the counter separated them. "What were you thinking of?"

The woman shrugged one slim shoulder. "Something . . . happy."

"Hmmm." She hesitated. "Most stories get terribly sad before they find their way to happy." She smiled, feeling the weight of the moment. "I'm Donna Barton. My story's like that."

For a few long seconds the woman looked at Donna, searching her eyes. "I'm Edna Carlton." Tears came quickly and fell onto her cheeks. She brushed at them with her fingers. "Sorry. I'm . . . still in the sad part."

Donna wanted to hug her or offer to pray for her. But she had a feeling that would come in time. "Want to talk about it?"

"No." She shook her head, adamant. "I . . . I'm sorry. Not today."

"That's fine." Donna nodded. "Someday . . . if you have time, I'll tell you mine."

Edna thought about that for a beat, and then the hint of a smile softened her expression. "I'd . . . like that."

"For now, though, let's find you a book." Donna came out from behind the counter and led Edna toward the classics. "Maybe something exciting. *The Adventures of Tom Sawyer*?"

"Hmm." Edna nodded slowly, lost in thought, the heartache strong in her eyes. "That might work." By the time she left the store with her book her tone was lighter, her mood not so heavy. She looked a little more able to face the world on the other side of The Bridge's front doors.

Whatever that world was for Edna Carlton.

When she was gone and after two newly regular customers filed into the store, Charlie found Donna again at the register. They were alone, the regulars out of sight. Charlie took her hands and looked at her for a long time. A thin layer of wetness shone in his eyes. "I miss her."

She didn't have to ask who he meant. "Me, too." She angled her head, seeing easily into his heart. "I never even saw her face."

"But you know what?" He smiled.

"What?" She closed the distance between them so their bodies were touching, their faces inches apart.

He looked over his shoulder to the place where the customers were chatting, clearly engaged in whatever book they were discussing. "One of those ladies back there is thinking about going into business. Know why?"

"Why?" Donna loved this, being in his arms, sharing a passion for The Bridge.

"Because of a book she bought here." His brow lifted, and his eyes grew even brighter. "A book changed her life, Donna." He looked around at the shelves of books, the walls they'd painted and the light fixtures they'd installed. "Because of our little bookstore. Because of The Bridge."

Donna felt the satisfaction to the depths of her soul. "The lady who was here earlier . . . she's hurting. But she'll be back. I sent her off with Tom Sawyer."

His smile faded and the dampness returned to his eyes. He released her hands and framed her face. "It's working."

"It is."

A sad laugh played on his lips. "I wasn't sure how to take my next breath." He spread his hands toward the books and walls that surrounded them. "God is so great . . . He hasn't forgotten us." He leaned in and kissed her slowly. A desperate kiss that reminded both of them how great the pain was that they were moving past.

His words stayed with her while she sorted through the cash register receipts later that day. How far they had come in the last few months. God was bringing the people who needed a bookstore, people who needed a connecting point, a way to see life through a clearer lens. People like Edna Carlton. Yes, He was bringing them a few more every day. Lives were being changed through the power of books. She and Charlie were giving their lives to make that possible. And along the way God was both healing them and using them.

Indeed, their plan really was working.

All because of The Bridge.

CHAPTER SIX

====================

Edna didn't rip into the book right away.

She let it sit on her kitchen counter like a stranger. When she would look at it between cups of coffee or moments of wandering through her apartment missing Tom, she had the feeling the book was looking back at her. Smiling at her.

Finally after her few dinner dishes were cleaned she picked it up and sat with it in the chair Tom liked best. She stared at the cover. Was it the title? The fact that Tom's name was a part of it? Something about the book called to her. Or maybe she felt this way because of the kind woman at the bookstore, the way she hadn't hesitated before leading her to this book. A book whose title contained the name of the man she missed so much.

Almost like Donna Barton had known exactly what she might need.

Edna opened the front cover. She knew the story, of course. But she had never actually read the book. The first words tugged at her heart and tears gathered in her eyes.

Aunt Polly was looking for Tom, but he wouldn't answer. No matter how long or loud she called him he wouldn't respond.

The way Edna had felt since the doorbell rang.

She blinked twice so she could see as she worked her way down the first page, and somehow despite her broken heart by the end of the third paragraph she was no longer sitting in a desperately quiet apartment wondering how she might keep on living. Rather she was in Aunt Polly's farmhouse grinning at the mischievous ways of young Tom.

A little like her own Tom had been back when he was in grade school.

When she finished the first chapter she kept reading, too caught up in the story to stop. Not until well after midnight did she close the book and set it on her bedside table. The next day at the mercantile she couldn't stop thinking about Tom and Huckleberry Finn and the trouble the two boys were getting into. The trouble they had survived, the plotting and planning of trouble yet ahead.

She could hardly wait to get home and pick up the book.

The story so captured her she forgot to eat until darkness fell outside, and when she finished the book in the wee hours of the morning she realized something she hadn't expected. Something other than Tom Carlton had consumed her for two full days.

The next afternoon when she was finished at the mercantile she hurried to The Bridge before the little shop closed. A sweet mix of rich coffee and worn leather filled the air and surrounded Edna. Donna was working at the counter again, and this time Edna walked up and gave the woman a hint of a curious smile. "How did you know?"

"Know what?" Donna's eyes were warm like before, warm and deeply concerned.

"*The Adventures of Tom Sawyer.* How did you know that's what I needed?"

"You said you were still at the sad part of your story. Tom Sawyer takes people out of their story and into his."

"The name. Tom." She didn't want to explain all of what happened, but she had to share this much. "That was my husband's name. He . . . was killed in Vietnam."

Sorrow welled up in Donna's eyes and after several seconds she came out from behind the counter. "Edna . . . I'm sorry." There was no hesitation now, no formalities between them. Donna hugged her and after a while she stepped back. "Whenever you want to talk about it, I'm here."

"Thank you." Edna sniffed. "I finished the book."

"Already?" Donna waited.

"I loved it. I was there on the river with them, sneaking around at night and slipping into the back of the church during the service." As she spoke, Edna's heart didn't feel as empty. "As long as I was reading the book, I . . ."

"You didn't notice your own story." Donna's eyes said she understood on a personal level.

"Exactly." Edna glanced at the shelves behind her. "I need another book." She turned and looked again at the gentle store owner. "But I'd like to hear your story first."

Donna's half smile was colored in a sadness that clearly still lived inside her. "Let's sit in the living room." The coffeepot was plugged in behind the front counter, quaint ceramic mugs stacked beside it. Donna poured them each a cup, gave one to Edna, and led the way to the worn leather sofa. They sat on opposite sides, facing each other. Donna took a slow breath, and for a long time she only waited, as if she were digging around in the basement of her heart for details she'd put behind her. A place where maybe she kept the story so she could get through the day.

Edna could certainly relate to that.

"It all started when I met Charlie Barton." This time her sweet smile touched her eyes. "I guess you could say God used Charlie to rescue me." She settled her shoulder into the sofa. "Before him my life was a nightmare." Her words came like a slow-motion flashback in a movie. She told of a childhood and adolescence marked by pain and loneliness, her parents' drug abuse and their early deaths.

No wonder she felt rescued when Charlie Barton came into her life.

Donna talked about Charlie's love of books and how his father wouldn't let him read. "Cement work was the only option as far as his dad was concerned. The two haven't spoken in some time."

Edna nodded, understanding. "That *is* sad."

"Actually . . . no." Donna narrowed her eyes and stared out a distant window at the back of the store. "The sad part is coming."

Edna took a sip of her coffee and felt her stomach tighten. She waited, determined not to interrupt the story again.

Donna went on about how she and Charlie got married and started life on their own—without any family. "We found out we were expecting much sooner than we planned." She looked at her hands folded on her lap, as if she were gathering strength for this next part. "Even so, we were happy. We didn't have family supporting us, so we figured God was letting us start one of our own."

She told about how smoothly her pregnancy had gone. But everything changed when she went into labor. Quiet tears slid down Donna's cheeks as she recounted the frightening medical emergency, the loss of her baby girl, and the reality that she could never have children.

Edna didn't realize until the end of the story that she was crying, too. Because she wasn't alone in her pain, in her sadness. People walking through the grocery store, and shopping at the mercantile, and even running a bookstore all had their own pain. Their own sad part of their story. She gave Donna's hand a squeeze, and let silence surround them for a minute. The two might be strangers, but they were not strangers to heartache.

They had that in common.

"So . . ." Edna kept her voice quiet, reverent, "you and Charlie moved to Franklin and opened The Bridge."

"Yes." Donna wiped the tears from her cheeks. She drank her coffee and seemed to wait while it worked through her. "God gave us this store. Here . . . we're finding our way back to happy." She put her hand on Edna's shoulder. "By putting books in the hands of people like you."

"Hmm. That's beautiful." She waited, not wanting to rush this time between them. "Thank you. For sharing."

"It helps." She sniffed, and the healing she'd experienced was evident in her eyes. "I'm here. When you want to talk about yours." She stood and nodded toward the rows of bookshelves. "Until then, let's get you another book."

Edna was glad Donna didn't push her. When she was ready to talk she had a feeling she would come here first. She and Donna walked a few aisles of fiction titles, more, Donna said, to give Edna a tour of the store. But the most natural next choice was an obvious one—*The Adventures of Huckleberry Finn.*

And so began a string of good days that continued as long as Edna was reading. Huck Finn gave way to a breathless chase after the husky Buck in *The Call of the Wild*. She was caught with the schoolboys on the deserted tropical island in *Lord of the Flies*, and her heart ached on the Oklahoma plains as she finished *The Grapes of Wrath*. She fell in love with Don Quixote and Rhett Butler and Jay Gatsby, and she fought alongside Captain Ahab against the white whale in *Moby-Dick*. A whale that came to represent her fear and loss.

With each new book she would share a cup of coffee with Donna at The Bridge, and gradually bits of her story, anecdotes from her childhood, came to the surface. After a few months of reading, Edna was a different person. She got out of bed easily and caught herself humming when she made her morning coffee.

Missing Tom was still a part of every breath, but her devastating heartache no longer consumed her. Books were changing her life. But she didn't consider the idea that they could do so much more.

That they might actually heal her.

===================

CHAPTER SEVEN

Edna could see something different in Donna's face as soon as she walked into The Bridge after work that day. It was summertime, and the city crowd from Nashville shopped Franklin's Main Street. More people meant more hours at the mercantile, so Edna made it into her favorite bookstore only once a week or so. This was one of those days.

Donna was waiting for her.

She smiled. "I picked out your next one." She pulled a book from beneath the register and set it on the counter. "It's time."

Edna and Donna were friends after so many months, but this was the first time the shopkeeper had ever chosen a book for her ahead of time. "Okay." Edna came closer and looked at the title. *Little Women.* She knew the story, of course, knew it was about a family of girls coming of age and she vaguely knew it was sad. That was the reason she'd avoided it. For all the books she'd allowed herself to get lost in, she'd avoided stories that dealt with great tragedy or loss.

After all, she was still in the middle of her own.

But looking at the cover, something about the book called to her. *Little Women*. She looked at Donna. Despite the time that had passed, she had never gone into detail about losing Tom. It was enough that her new friend had the facts. The rest of the story would come in time. When the thought of recounting it didn't make Edna feel sick.

Donna held out the book. "It's about loss. I won't hide the fact." Tucked in her expression was a wisdom greater than her twenty-something years, a wisdom that could only have come from experience. Edna hadn't noticed that about the shopkeeper before. "Read it . . . please."

Something in her tone left Edna no option. She began the book that night and immediately became part of the March family. As she traveled the chapters, her deep connection to the characters had her laughing one minute and touched the next. She could see where the story was going. *Little Women* had been around as long as Edna could remember. Some of her friends had to read it in English class, but Edna's teacher had assigned an anthology of short stories instead.

Not only had she missed this brilliant and beautiful story, but she had missed the reason it was sad. By the time she realized the inevitable tragedy just ahead, Edna was a fifth sister and sweet Beth was her best friend. As Beth's frailty became more evident and her condition worsened, Edna read the book through streams of tears.

After three days of reading, Edna sat beside Beth and watched her tender musical heart gracefully begin to slip away. When Beth drew her last breath, Edna wept uncontrollably, the way she had given way to sobs after Tom's death. Questions railed against her soul. Why did people have to die? And why was it always the good ones, the kind ones like Beth and Tom? Why didn't God take the liars and crooks first? She mourned with the March family, and somehow she felt they were mourning with her, too. Not only mourning their Beth.

But mourning Edna's Tom. The whole March family.

At first she was angry at Donna for giving her the book. How could it ever be time to immerse herself in such a sad story? For a week she avoided The Bridge, avoided telling Donna how far back reading *Little Women* had set her. But the story stayed in her heart, calling to her, and a day after she finished it, she read it again. Faster this time. And one late night she came upon a line that took her breath away. Like a lightbulb turning on in Edna's soul, something happened inside her. She read the line over and over again.

Love is the only thing that we can carry with us when we go, and it makes the end so easy.

Suddenly Edna knew without any doubt that it had been like this for Tom. He had taken her love with him, and so when death called, he had been able to go. The God he loved had called him home, and he had gone easily. Because he could take Edna's love with him.

She closed the book and walked to her bedside table where she still kept Tom's T-shirt. It felt soft in her hands, and she pressed it to her face. She hadn't slept with it in a while. Whatever book she read at night had replaced her need for it. But now . . . now she breathed in the faint smell of him again. And deep inside her she felt the gaping wounds of losing him begin to heal.

Tom still loved her. He carried her love with him.

The next day she went to the department store and picked out a beautiful scrapbook. One with a textured canvas cover and a space in the middle for a single photo. Edna knew just the one that would work for the gift. Borrowing a camera from the owner of the mercantile, she took three pictures of The Bridge. She still didn't go inside. That could wait until she finished putting together the gift.

When she picked up the finished prints, she chose one that seemed to capture the bookstore better than the others. She placed it carefully in the framed window at the center of the scrapbook cover and smoothed her hand over it.

Perfect.

Next, she opened the cover, and on the inside flap she wrote:

Donna . . . Fill this book with the stories of old souls like me. People who sometimes need a place like this to bridge yesterday and tomorrow. People looking for a second chance. Thank you!

She wrapped the gift and the next day she took it to The Bridge.

CHAPTER EIGHT

Edna was a little concerned.

So much time had passed since she'd been to The Bridge that she wondered if Donna might be cool with her, distant. But as she stepped inside the bookstore, the shopkeeper's smile was the first thing she saw. Immediately, Donna came from behind the counter and hugged her. For a long time she looked in her eyes, as if she were checking Edna's heart for fresh scars. "You read it."

"I did." Edna handed her the wrapped scrapbook. "This is for you." She hesitated. "Before you open it . . . can we talk?"

Donna only smiled and poured them each a cup of coffee. "I was expecting this."

How the young shopkeeper was so wise, Edna could only imagine. But as she took her cup of coffee and sat again with Donna on the sofa, her entire story spilled from her heart. They both cried when she got to the part about the doorbell ringing. When she finished, she looked at Donna for a long time. "You knew."

"Yes. God told me you needed that book."

Edna narrowed her eyes, puzzled. "God?" Not since Tom had she met someone who talked about the Lord like He was her friend. But He must have told Donna. The healing that had started in Edna's heart made it impossible to question her friend's certainty.

"Our faith and this store . . . that's how we survived." Donna gave Edna a lingering side hug. "We prayed we'd meet people like you. Hurting people who needed God and a good book. So they'd have a chance to survive."

"People like me." Edna understood now.

"Exactly."

"After that day, October fifth, I didn't think I'd survive. I thought—"

"Wait." Donna stared at her. "October fifth?"

"Yes. The day I got the news about Tom."

"Edna . . . that's the same day . . . the day our little girl died."

The truth of that took a long time to settle in, and for a good bit they were quiet, the air around them almost holy. Edna drank her coffee, marveling over the mystery and about Donna's prayer and how God had answered it. She nodded to the package. "You can open it now."

"You didn't have to . . ."

"I wanted to do more."

Donna gingerly ripped the paper from the gift, and for a long time she just stared at the cover. She ran her fingertips over the photo, and after a few seconds one tear and then another hit the canvas.

"It's a scrapbook . . . I wrote you something inside."

Donna opened the cover carefully, and Edna watched her read the inscription. Finally she lifted teary eyes to Edna, and again she leaned close and hugged her. "Thank you. We don't have anything like this. A way to track the names and faces God brings through the door."

Edna couldn't help but think that in some ways the scrapbook would take the place of the baby books and yearbooks and family photo albums Donna and Charlie would never have. Donna seemed to be thinking the same thing, because once more she looked at the cover, and then she thumbed her way through the empty pages, as if she could see the way they might be filled in the years and decades to come.

"It needs one thing. A picture of you beneath what you wrote." Donna set her coffee cup down on an end table and hurried back toward the register. She pulled a camera from one of the adjacent cupboards. "Do you have your book? *Little Women*?"

Edna grinned. "In my purse." She took it with

her everywhere. Already she was on her third time through it.

"Let's see." Donna surveyed the area. "Stay there. This is perfect. The light from the back window is straight on you." Her tone was lighter, more full of life. "Hold your book like you're reading it."

The woman's enthusiasm was contagious. Edna found her copy of *Little Women*, crossed her legs, and held the novel open on her lap, opened to her favorite page, her favorite quote. It was the only one with the corner of the page bent over.

Love is the only thing that we can carry with us when we go, and it makes the end so easy.

She felt a sad smile fill her heart and move to her lips. The quote would stay with her always. As she looked at it, she didn't hear Donna taking the picture until it was over.

"There. Years from now when I'm an old lady, that picture . . . that's how I'll always remember you, Edna."

"Donna, you won't need to remember me. I'll still be sitting in that chair reading whatever book you put in my hands."

Donna held up the camera. "I like that picture even better than the one I just took."

The next half hour passed quickly, and Edna had to get to work. When she stopped in a few days later, the scrapbook was on the counter for everyone to see.

And the photograph Donna had taken was pasted in the scrapbook right where she said she was going to put it: beneath Edna's words.

Edna had a feeling that someday when she looked back, the scrapbook—and the picture of herself with her precious copy of *Little Women*—would mean as much to her as it would to Donna. Suddenly a realization hit her, one that filled her with indescribable joy.

She had just now been thinking about the future! Not tomorrow or next week. But years from now. Thinking about it without fear or worry or dread. And without wondering how she was going to survive without Tom Carlton. Which could only mean one thing: Though she would never stop missing her husband, she was healing.

She was going to make it.

Because of the Bartons and The Bridge and a handful of books including one that her friend, Donna, had somehow known she needed. The one God wanted her to read.

Louisa May Alcott's *Little Women*.

———

Donna waited until Edna was gone before she called Charlie to the front of the store. He loved the scrapbook as much as she did, but he hadn't seen the developed picture of Edna yet.

"Look at this." Donna motioned Charlie to her side. "Our first photograph in the scrapbook." She opened the front cover and showed him her work.

"Hmmm." Charlie leaned closer. "That's her, all right. The look in her eyes . . . like she's captured by the story."

"She was." Donna smiled at the picture of her new friend. "She didn't hear me click the camera."

"Fills my heart, Donna . . . This is what we wanted with The Bridge."

"Yes." She turned to him and put her hands on his shoulders. "You're a brilliant businessman, Charlie. Your father was wrong."

Gratitude shone in his eyes. "I love you."

She leaned close and kissed him. "You were born for this."

"We both were."

For a few seconds they were quiet, and Donna wondered if, like her, he was thinking about their little girl. "Say something."

"I don't cry in the early morning anymore. Thinking about her."

"Charlie . . ." She framed his face with her hand, his cheek rough against her fingers. "I thought I was the only one."

"I saw her, Donna. I held her little body." He clenched his jaw, clearly fighting a fresh kind of sadness. "I'll always miss her."

They swayed a little, drawing strength from each other, from a love deeper than most. Charlie looked down at the scrapbook. "You know what I think when I see that book . . . those empty pages?" He linked his arms gently around her waist. "I think about all the faces we're yet to meet, the people who will come through the doors. Folks who need a good book and someone who cares."

"God will bring them. He brought Edna."

"Yes, He did." This time he kissed her, more slowly than before. "Thank you, Donna . . . for believing in me."

"Always, Charlie . . ." She put her head on his chest and held onto him. The way she would as long as she lived. "Always."

With that, Charlie whispered a prayer. He thanked God for His faithfulness, and he asked Him to keep the doors of The Bridge open for many, many decades. Charlie closed by asking that the Lord might bring people who needed something to get them from the pain of yesterday to the possibility of tomorrow. People who needed God and the two of them. And the miracle of a small-town bookstore.

So that some far-off day the scrapbook would no longer be empty.

It would be overflowing.

the
BRIDGE

Other Life-Changing Fiction™
by Karen Kingsbury

BAILEY FLANIGAN SERIES
Leaving
Learning
Longing
Loving

9/11 SERIES
One Tuesday Morning
Beyond Tuesday Morning
Remember Tuesday Morning

LOST LOVE SERIES
Even Now
Ever After

ABOVE THE LINE SERIES
Above the Line: Take One
Above the Line: Take Two
Above the Line: Take Three
Above the Line: Take Four

STAND-ALONE TITLES
Oceans Apart
Between Sundays

When Joy Came to Stay
On Every Side
Divine
Like Dandelion Dust
Where Yesterday Lives
Shades of Blue
Unlocked
Coming Home—The Baxter
   Family

REDEMPTION SERIES
Redemption
Remember
Return
Rejoice
Reunion

FIRSTBORN SERIES
Fame
Forgiven
Found
Family
Forever

www.KarenKingsbury.com
Twitter: @KarenKingsbury
Facebook: AuthorKarenKingsbury

the
BRIDGE

A NOVEL

Karen Kingsbury

HOWARD BOOKS
A DIVISION OF SIMON & SCHUSTER, INC.
New York   Nashville   London   Toronto   Sydney   New Delhi

Howard Books
A Division of Simon & Schuster, Inc.
1230 Avenue of the Americas
New York, NY 10020

First Howard Books hardcover edition October 2012

HOWARD and colophon are trademarks of Simon & Schuster, Inc.

Designed by Jaime Putorti

Manufactured in the United States of America

ISBN 978-1-4516-4701-3   The Bridge
ISBN for dual edition: 978-1-62090-807-5

Scripture quotations taken from The Holy Bible, New International Version® (NIV®). Copyright © 1973, 1978, 1984 by Biblica US, Inc.®. Used by permission.

Published in association with the literary agency of Alive Communications, Inc., 7680 Goddard Street, Suite 200, Colorado Springs, CO 80920, www.alive communications.com.

To Donald, my Prince Charming . . .

Another year behind us, and already Tyler is almost finished with his first year at Liberty University while Kelsey is taking wing—acting in films that glorify God. Isn't our Lord so faithful? Not just with our kids, but in leading our family where He wants us to be. Closing in on a year in Nashville, and it's so very clear that God wanted us here. Thank you for being so steady and strong and good and kind. Hold my hand and walk with me through the coming seasons . . . the graduations and growing up and getting older. All of it's possible with you by my side. I love you always and forever.

To Kyle, my newest son . . .

Kyle, you and Kelsey are married now, and forevermore we will see you as our son, as the young man God planned for our daughter, the one we've prayed for and talked to God about and hoped for. Your heart is beautiful in every way, Kyle. How you cherish simple moments and the way you are kind beyond words. You see the good in people and situations, and you find a way to give God the glory always. I will never forget you coming to me and Donald at different times and telling us that you wanted to support Kelsey and keep her safe . . . and ultimately that you wanted to love her all the days of your life. All of it is summed up in the way you do one simple action: The way you look at our precious Kelsey. It's a picture that will hang forever on the wall of my heart. You look at Kelsey like nothing and no one else in all the world exists but her. In your eyes at that moment is the picture of what love looks like. Kyle, as God takes you from one stage to another—using that beautiful voice of yours to glorify Him and lead others to love Jesus— I pray that you always look at Kelsey the way you do today. We thank God for you, and we look forward to the beautiful seasons ahead. Love you always!

To Kelsey, my precious daughter . . .

What a joy to see you blossom here in Nashville, Kels! How grateful I am that this is a season of love and laughter and friendship like you've never known before. As you said, God is faithful. Live for Him and watch how He will bless you. How great that you are experiencing that firsthand, newly married to Kyle, the man of your dreams. So glad that in this season you're close to home, still the light of our family, the laughter in our hearts. I pray God will bless you and Kyle mightily in the years to come. In the meantime, you'll be in my heart every moment. And wherever you sing and dance and act for Him, we'll be in the front row! I love you, sweetheart.

To Tyler, my lasting song . . .

Some of my favorite moments since you left for college are when we gather around the kitchen computer and talk to you on Skype. I love that in those moments you slip into your funny self, making us laugh until we cry and pretending to be every cut-up character that comes to your mind. But while you can still make us laugh, you are growing into such an amazing godly young man. Your blog, Ty's Take, is being followed by readers who long to know how God is working in your life while you're at college. Your dad and I are so proud of you, Ty. We're proud of your talent and your compassion for people and your place in our family. However your dreams unfold, we'll be cheering loudest as we watch them happen. Hold on to Jesus, son. I love you.

To Sean, my happy sunshine . . .

You are growing up and listening to God's lead, and in the process you are taking your studies and your homework so much more seriously. God will bless you for how you're being faithful in the little things, Sean. He has such great plans ahead for you. Remember, home is where your heart is always safe. Keep working . . . keep pushing . . . keep believing. Go to bed every night knowing you did all you could to prepare yourself for the doors God will open in the days ahead. I pray that as you soar for the Lord, He will allow you to be a very bright light indeed. You're a precious gift, son. Keep smiling and keep seeking God's best.

To Josh, my tenderhearted perfectionist . . .

Soccer was where you started when you first came here from Haiti, and soccer is the game that God seems to be opening up for you. In a number of ways God is showing you that through soccer, you can be a very bright light for Him. But as proud as I am of your athleticism, I'm most proud of your growth this past year. You've grown in heart, maturity, kindness, quiet strength, and the realization that time at home is short. God is going to use you for great things, and I believe He'll put you on a public platform to do it. Stay strong in Him, and listen to His quiet whispers so you'll know which direction to turn. I'm so proud of you, son—I'll forever be cheering on the sidelines. Keep God first in your life. I love you always.

To EJ, my chosen one . . .

EJ, I wish you could know just how much we love you and how deeply we believe in the great plans God has for you. One day not too far from here, you'll be applying to colleges, thinking about the career choices ahead of you, the path God might be leading you down. Wherever that path takes you, keep your eyes on Jesus, and you'll always be as full of possibility as you are today. I expect great things from you, EJ, and I know the Lord does, too. I'm so glad you're a part of our family, always and forever. I love you more than you know. I'm praying you'll have a strong passion to use your gifts for God as you move through your sophomore year. Thanks for your giving heart, EJ. I love you so.

To Austin, my miracle boy . . .

Austin, I love that you care enough to be and do your best. It shows in your straight A's and it shows in the way you treat your classmates. Of course, it absolutely shows when you play any sport. Always remember what I've told you about that determination. Let it push you to be better, but never, ever let it discourage you. You're so good at life, Austin. Keep the passion and keep that beautiful faith of yours. Every single one of your dreams is within reach. Keep your eyes on Him, and we'll keep our eyes on you, our youngest son. There is nothing more sweet than cheering you boys on—and for you, that happened from the time you were born, through your heart surgery until now. I thank God for you, for the miracle of your life. I love you, Austin.

And to God Almighty, the Author of Life,
who has — for now — blessed me with these.

CHAPTER ONE

She should have said something.

Even now, seven years later, with Thanksgiving dishes put away and another lonely December rushing up at her, Molly Allen knew the truth. Her year, her life, her Christmas . . . all of it might be different if only she'd said something.

The possibilities plagued her that Black Friday. They walked with her through the front door of her Portland, Oregon, private foundation office, hovered beside her over lunch at P.F. Changs, and distracted her every time she stopped in to see the cats and dogs at her animal rescue shelter.

This was Video Day. Molly's day after Thanksgiving.

Everyone else in the greater Portland area spent the day hunting bargains and stopping in at her shelter to see if the gift they wanted might be in a cage instead of a Walmart. But now, as the day wound down, while shoppers unpacked their bags and counted their savings, Molly would snuggle beneath a blanket by herself and watch the video.

The way she did every year on this day.

She tucked a strand of long blond hair behind her ear and stooped down to the oversize cage on the bottom row. The room echoed with a dozen different barks and whimpers and cries for attention. A chorus of unrest and slight concern from the animals rescued this month to her shelter, one arm of the Allen Foundation's efforts.

"Okay, Buster." She unlatched the cage and welcomed a curly-haired gray terra-poo into her arms. "It's your lucky day. Yes, it is." She snapped a leash to Buster's collar. The dog was a two-year-old, stuck at the shelter for three weeks. Longer than usual, considering this was Christmastime, and the cute dogs usually went first. She scratched the dog just above his ear. "Let's get you to your family."

For good measure, she made a general announcement to the others. "It's still seven days till December, gang. Your turn will come!"

Buster wagged his tail furiously as Molly led him to the lobby. She liked Buster's new family. Of course, she liked most families. Anyone willing to rescue a pet was a friend of hers, no question. But this family with their twin seven-year-old boys seemed special. Their eyes lit up as Molly rounded the corner with Buster.

"Daddy, that's him! Our Buster dog!" One of the boys ran up and dropped to his knees, hugging Buster around his neck.

The other boy was quieter and hung back by their parents. His grin brightened the room all the same. The family had already signed the necessary paperwork, so this was the last step. Both parents shook her hand as they left. "What you're doing here, it's making a difference." The dad's eyes were warm. "I have a feeling you could be doing many more things with your time." He nodded at her. "Merry Christmas."

"Thank you." Molly hesitated. "Happy holidays."

The family turned their attention to Buster and the excitement of getting him out the door in the pouring rain and into their van parked just outside. As the family drove off, Molly checked the time. Six minutes till closing. She walked to the door and flipped the sign. The cages were clean, and the animals all exercised by ten volunteer high school kids who had worked until an hour ago. She would check the water bowls and head home.

———————

He called the video project "The Bridge."

Somewhere in the opening credits, he wrote this descriptor: *How a small-town boy from Carthage, Mississippi, and a highbrow girl from Pacific Heights, California, found common ground on a daily commute down Franklin Road outside Music City to The Bridge—the best little bookstore in the world.*

Too wordy, too many locations, Molly had told him. The two of them would laugh about how he ever could've gotten an A on the assignment with such a horrific descriptor.

Molly set her drenched things down just inside the door of her walk-up apartment, turned on the lights, and took off her dripping raincoat. She lived well below her means, in a new two-bedroom unit on the famous NW Twenty-third Street. Trees along Twenty-third sparkled with twinkling lights even in July, and the street boasted local coffee shops, cafés, and boutiques with only-in-Portland art and fashion. The pace and people took the edge off.

Her father would have hated it.

Dinner simmered in the Crock-Pot, vegetable potato soup with fresh-diced leeks and garlic and parsley. The soup he taught her to make. Her Black Friday soup. A whiny meow came from the laundry room, and her cat Sam strolled up, rubbing against her ankles. He was a funny cat. More dog than feline. "Hi, Sam."

He flopped down on the kitchen floor and put his head between his paws.

"Exhausted, are you?" She bent down and scratched beneath his chin. "Good boy, Sam. Don't overdo it."

She ladled out a small bowlful of soup, grabbed her blanket and the remote control and settled into one half of her leather loveseat. The top button on the remote dimmed the lights, and the next would start the movie, which had been in the player since early that morning.

Molly caught her hair in her hands and pulled it to one side.

His name was Ryan Kelly.

Now he was married to the sweet Southern belle he'd dated back in high school, no doubt teaching music at Carthage High in Nowhere, Mississippi. But for two years while they attended Belmont University, Ryan had been hers. She'd dreamed of never going home again and playing violin for the philharmonic, and he'd talked about touring with a country band, making music on his guitar for a living. In the end, he had Kristen, his Southern girl back home, and Molly had her dad's empire to run in San Francisco.

But for those four sweet semesters at the Franklin bookstore, nothing came between them.

The ending was the hardest, the final touch, the turning away, her trembling hands. Every gut-wrenching heartbeat remained etched in her soul forever. Their good-bye had happened so fast, she still wasn't sure she understood why. How they could've parted ways so quickly and finally.

Molly hit the play button, and as the music began, the familiar ache built inside her. She didn't often allow herself this trip back to then. But the day after Thanksgiving belonged to him, to the way things once were, and to the unavoidable, inescapable truth.

Like Rhett Butler in *Gone with the Wind,* she should've said something.

———————

He had set the camera up on the dashboard, rigged it with masking tape and a dowel so he could turn it slightly. The viewfinder flipped out, facing them. "Just act natural," he told her. "Keep your eyes on the road." His taped laughter rang through her living room the way it once rang through her mornings and afternoons.

The video started with the camera on him, and his first question always made her smile. "Okay, Miss Molly, tell the people how we met. The unlikely meeting that started the madness."

"The whole story?" He had turned the camera so she came into view, her face less than agreeable as she drove her BMW sedan. "While we're driving?"

He laughed again. "It's thirty minutes to The Bridge. I think you can multitask."

She made a face at him and then laughed as she glanced at the camera. "Fine. What's the question again?"

"Keep your eyes on the road."

Their laughter came together in an up-tempo waltz, while the camera caught the discreet way their bodies seemed drawn to each other. The slight but intentional way their knees and elbows brushed together and the way she looked at him as he filmed her—as if she'd never been happier in all her life. Molly smiled as the video played. The camera had caught their heart connection, the friendship definitely, but it had also caught the connection they hadn't been willing to talk about. The chemistry between them, so strong it took her breath even now.

Their crazy undeniable chemistry.

As the video played on, something remarkable happened, the reason Molly watched the video every year on this day. She no longer felt herself sitting in front of her TV screen watching footage shot seven years ago. Instead she was there again, the sun on her shoulders, adventure in her heart, the summer after her high school graduation. Not in a flashback sort of way. But really there. Heading into an oversize auditorium with three brand-new girlfriends for August orientation at Belmont.

Maybe it was the sense of freedom Molly felt that

day, the fact that she'd convinced her father to let her do the unthinkable—leave the West Coast to attend college in a flyover state like Tennessee. Or the fact that here she wasn't an heiress biding time until she could take over her father's corporation. She was a college kid, same as everyone else. Whatever it was, that day she felt wonderfully alive and hopeful, every predictable aspect of her life as far removed as the Pacific Ocean.

That day the Belmont auditorium was filled with the energy of college freshmen excited and anxious and desperately trying to fit in. Molly and the girls took the first open seats. Her eyes had barely adjusted to the light in the auditorium when one of her friends nudged the other. "Look at him!" She pointed to a guy one section over. He was tall and built, with short dark hair and piercing blue eyes. "He's looking at me!"

"Nice try." The friend laughed. "He's looking at Molly. Same as every other guy."

"Don't be ridiculous. He's just . . ." Molly giggled, but she couldn't finish her thought. Because in those few seconds, the connection between her and the dark-haired freshman was so strong it took her breath. She'd met a number of kids by then—through registration and lunch and field games earlier that afternoon. This felt different, and Molly knew one thing without a doubt, no matter what else happened in her four years at Belmont.

She would never forget this single moment.

They didn't talk, didn't make their way toward each other when orientation finished that evening. Molly almost wondered if her dad had someone following her, someone who would pay the guy to stay out of her way. Because her time here had come with a stipulation from her parents. She could study music, but she couldn't date. If her father found out she was seeing a Belmont boy, he would bring her home on the next flight.

"You'll marry your own kind," he always told her. He'd say it with a smile, but he was serious all the same. And he didn't mean she'd marry just any guy in their circle of friends.

He meant Preston J. Millington III.

Preston had attended boarding school with her. The guy was smart and kind and personable enough. Their parents were best friends, and Preston was on the fast track for an MBA. Her father had already

promised him a position with his shipping corporation.

Molly had no feelings for Preston, but she'd been
raised to believe she didn't have a choice. No say in
the decisions that would shape her life. Not until she
set foot on the Belmont campus did her life feel re-
motely like it was her own. Still, by the end of the first
week of school, Molly wondered if she'd ever see the
boy from orientation again.

That Friday one of Molly's friends invited her over
for dinner, and she said yes, the way she said yes to
every invite. She loved the freedom of coming and
going whenever she wanted and spending time with
people regardless of their income and influence. Her
friend lived in downtown Franklin, thirty minutes
south of Nashville. As Molly stepped out of her
sedan, she saw a guy climb out of an old Dodge
truck at the house next door. He had a guitar case
slung over his back, and he stopped cold when he
spotted her.

Again their eyes met, and Molly leaned on her
open car door. It was him, she had no doubt. But what
was he doing here? Before she could ask his name or
why he was there, half an hour from campus, or what

classes he was taking, her friend bounded out the front door. "Molly! You're here! Come in and meet everyone. My mom's been cooking all day and—"

Molly pulled herself away from his deep stare and hugged her friend. They were halfway up the walk when she turned back and looked for him, but he must've gone inside. All through dinner, Molly thought about him, thinking up ways to ask her friend's family who he was and whether he lived there or if he was visiting.

When she left that night, his truck was gone.

But on Monday, Molly arrived early to the music building for her instrumental theory class. As she entered the hallway, she was practically overcome by the beautiful sounds of an acoustic guitar and a guy singing a song she'd never heard. His voice melted her, and somehow even before she rounded the corner into the room, she knew. As if she'd known him all her life, she knew.

Seeing him on the other side of the classroom door only confirmed it.

He smiled and kept playing, kept singing, while she leaned against the wall and watched. When the song ended, he lowered his guitar and looked right through her. "I was beginning to think you were a figment of my imagination."

She tried to think of a witty response, but her laughter came first. "You're a music student?"

"I am." He stood and shook her hand with his free one. This close, his eyes looked bluer than they had in the auditorium. "Ryan Kelly. They had me in the wrong class. Just got it all worked out."

"So you're in here?" Her heart soared.

"If I can catch up." He gave her a half grin and raised his brow. "I might have a few questions."

She felt her eyes start to dance. "I might have the answers."

And like that, it started.

Neither of them lived on campus. He couldn't afford the room and board, so he lived in Franklin with an older couple, family friends. She lived in a house her parents owned in Brentwood's McGavock Farms. Her dad had bought it well below market value. He hired a crew to renovate it before school started, with plans to keep it until she left Belmont, when he would sell it for a profit. For now the house was staffed with a housekeeper and groundsman, a married couple who lived upstairs. Molly had a suite on the main floor, adjacent to the music room, where she could practice and study. Dorm living was out of the question.

"Communal living is not suitable," her dad had told her. He tried to soften his expression. "You don't know anything about that lifestyle. This way you'll be safe."

From the beginning, her feelings for Ryan were anything but safe. And since her parents' staff would've reported her for having a boy over, Ryan's idea was perfect from the beginning. "I know of this bookstore. New and used books in an old house in downtown Franklin. It has a reading room upstairs that no one uses. My home away from home." He smiled at her, and the sparkle in his eyes touched the depths of her soul. "It's called The Bridge."

Molly was intrigued, and from that first study session, The Bridge became a private world for Ryan and her, a hiding place for the two of them. Sure, there were other patrons, but Belmont students didn't drive that far, and Molly loved the anonymity.

The store was set up in an old house that once was a hiding place for Union soldiers during the Civil War. The floors were old weathered pine, and the walls and doors had settled so that they didn't quite line up. The place smelled of old books and rich leather, and Molly loved everything about it.

The Bridge was run by a man named Charlie Barton, a friend to the people of Franklin. Charlie kept fresh-brewed coffee on a table near the front register where he hung out, quick with the right suggestion of a book or an insightful conversation. Once in a while his wife, Donna, joined him. The couple would sit with Molly and Ryan near the fireplace and listen. Really listen.

"Tell me about your classes," Charlie would say. Then he'd pull up a chair as if he had all day to hear details about music lectures and science tests and the English lit reports they were working on.

Donna would sometimes pull Molly aside. "That boy's in love with you," she'd say. "When are you both going to admit it?"

Molly would laugh. "We're just friends. Seriously."

"Hmm." Donna would raise her eyebrows. "I guess we'll see."

By the end of the first semester, Molly felt closer to Charlie and Donna than she felt to her own parents.

"I'm never going back," she told Ryan more than

one afternoon while they were at The Bridge. "They can't make me."

He would grin at her, his eyes shining in a way that stayed with her still. "No one can make us do anything."

It took only a few study dates to learn all there was to know about each other. Molly told him things she hadn't told anyone. How her life back home suffocated her and how she had never considered crossing her parents or disobeying them. She told him about Preston and her father's corporation and the plans he had for her.

He was honest, too. "I have a girlfriend back in Carthage." He watched her, looking for a reaction. "We've dated since our sophomore year of high school. Our families attend the same church."

Molly felt the sting of the news, but she didn't let him see. She couldn't date him, anyway. He would be her friend, nothing more. Knowing about his girlfriend back home only made him safer, giving her permission to get as close to him as she wanted.

In the beginning, Ryan talked about his girlfriend fairly often. "Her dad's a farmer," he told Molly one day when they were studying at The Bridge. "He's giving her two acres, so later . . . you know, we can live there."

Molly nodded, thoughtful. She didn't look away, didn't waver in her connection to him. "How will you be a professional guitar player in Carthage, Mississippi?"

His quiet chuckle was colored with discouragement. "I wouldn't be. Everyone thinks I'll come back and teach music at the high school."

"What about you?" Her voice grew softer, the quiet of the store's living room encouraging the conversation. "What do you want?"

"It's a good Plan B, teaching music. I like Carthage."

It hit her then how much they had in common, their lives already planned out. Suddenly she couldn't stand the thought. "No, Ryan!" She took hold of his shoulder and gave it a gentle squeeze. "You can't settle. You have to go for Plan A. Tour the world with the top country bands and play that beautiful guitar of yours."

"Me?" He laughed again, but his eyes showed a hint of adventure that hadn't been there before. "What about you? None of this Preston and San Francisco for you, Molly Allen. You have to play violin for the philharmonic." His laughter faded, and he'd never looked more serious. "No matter what they want for you."

Like that, their dreams were set. They promised to push each other, to never settle for anything but the place where their hearts led. They took turns commuting to Belmont, and they shared a ride every day from the beginning. Ryan would pull his truck up at the corner of McGavock Farms and Murray, where she'd be waiting, out of sight of the staff. He'd take her to school and then to The Bridge when classes were done.

Homework wasn't all they did at The Bridge. They also found books, classics that spoke deeply to them. *Gone with the Wind* and her favorite, Charlotte Brontë's *Jane Eyre*. From the beginning Molly related to the heroine and her determination to do the right thing, even at the cost of love. They read *Jane Eyre* aloud to each other, and once in a while, on the drive to The Bridge, they would quote lines to each other.

"'I'm asking what Jane Eyre would do to secure my happiness,'" Ryan would say in his best English accent, quoting Rochester.

"'I would do anything for you, sir,'" she would

quote Jane in her own Victorian accent, stifling the giggles that always came when they were together. "'Anything that was right.'"

When they weren't quoting Brontë's novel, they sang along with the radio and talked about their classes and dreamed of the future. For two wonderful years they never talked about the one thing that seemed so obvious at the time, the thing that could've made all the difference. They never talked about whether their friendship was a cover for the obvious.

That maybe they were in love with each other.

As the video wound down and Sam curled up on the floor beside her, as her tears slid down her cheeks the way they did every time she watched the film, Molly couldn't help but think the one thing she would always think this time of year.

She should've said something.

CHAPTER TWO

Charlie Barton sank into the worn refinished leather sofa and looked around the empty walls of The Bridge. Even stripped bare, the place was home. But for how much longer? He closed his eyes and tried to still his trembling hands, tried to find a reason to believe again.

Please, God . . . show me the way. I'm out of answers.

He waited, but there was no response, no whispered words of hope or gentle reminders or inspiring Scripture. Nothing. *Are You there, God? Are You really there?* With all of his strength, he fought the ocean of tears rising up inside his soul. He was out of money, and the latest loan hadn't come through. He couldn't buy books to stock his store without at least a line of credit. And no books meant no store.

Another wave of despair washed up against the shore of his soul. All he could see was the way Donna had looked at him when he left home an hour ago— like even *she'd* lost faith in him.

After thirty years in downtown Franklin, Charlie understood the gravity of the situation. Like so many bookstores across the country, his was about to become a casualty. Not because of e-readers—Charlie had enough customers who wanted a real book in their hands. But because of something totally out of his control.

The hundred-year flood.

Charlie opened his eyes and leaned forward, digging his elbows into his knees and placing his hands over his weathered face. The floodwaters had come swift and relentless, nearly twenty inches of rain in two days. He hadn't packed up the books. There hadn't been time. If he'd known how bad it would get, he might've come here anyway, risking his life if that's what it took. By the time he thought about clearing out the store, he would've needed a boat to get to The Bridge.

The water had broken through the windows and knocked over shelves, taking even the books that might've been out of reach of the rising flood. Every book. Every single book was either swept away or left in the corners of the store, mushy piles of pulp. Only the furniture remained, and it was too damaged to save. His insurance policy on the store's contents didn't cover a tenth of what he'd invested in books. No, the flood left nothing. With a clean sweep, it removed all that Charlie Barton had spent his life working for, everything that had mattered to him.

Everything but his faith in God and his lovely Donna.

He looked up and squinted through the fading light out the storefront window. What would Franklin be without a bookstore? Without a place where people could come to learn about history and explorations, fiction and political figures? Where would they go to talk about their ideas and experience the feel of a book in their hands? The weight of the binding and smell of the ink, the feel of the paper between their fingers and the sound of turning pages.

A real book.

Charlie gritted his teeth and worked the muscles in his jaw. This wasn't the end. He closed his eyes again. God wouldn't have brought him this far to see him fail, right? Certainly not. He ran through the options one more time, and his burst of confidence dimmed. He hadn't told Donna about the loan.

The bells on the front door jingled and he looked up. The sign out front said he was reopening on December 8—not ideal but still well before Christmas. The bells on the front door and the worn sofa were the only purchases he'd made so far. He watched as the door opened and Donna walked in. At fifty-six, she was still pretty, still petite, with a girlish face that he loved more with each passing year.

"Charlie." She came to him, her expression weary but patient. "How long are you going to sit here?"

"Until they make me leave." His smile felt heavy, and his eyes blurred, the unshed tears finding a way. "You didn't have to come."

"I did." She helped him to his feet and took him in her arms. "The bank called."

His heart sank. He'd wanted to tell her himself. He drew back and searched her eyes. "What'd they say?"

"The line of credit was denied."

Charlie lowered his gaze to his old brown loafers, the ones he'd worn to The Bridge every day for five years. The business had never been lucrative. He and

Donna had sacrificed to keep the place, but neither of them would've changed a thing. The Bridge gave them a purpose. He was quiet for a long while.

"Donna . . ." His voice cracked. He looked at her, his heart aching with sadness. "It was worth it, right?"

"What?" She had hold of his hands now, her eyes kinder than he deserved.

"The Bridge, the bookstore . . . all the years." He touched her hair, her cheek. "You never had nice things. We never traveled."

She looked at him for a long time and then put her hands on his shoulders. "Our time here, it was never about the money. It was about the people." She pointed out the front window. "There's not a person in Franklin who hasn't been touched by your books and your kindness, Charlie Barton."

He let the words soak in and then pulled her close once more. "I don't deserve you." They stayed that way for half a minute, rocking slightly to the sound of their beating hearts and the passing cars and pedestrians outside. Finally, he took a step back and shrugged. "What should we do?"

For the first time since she walked into the store, her face clouded. "That's just it, Charlie." She crossed her arms and turned her back to him, her eyes on the empty spaces. It took her nearly a minute to face him again. "No matter how many people you've touched, they won't pay the bills. Your customers can't buy books we don't have."

He waited, hoping she had something else, some way out that he'd missed.

Instead she looked down for a long moment. When she lifted her eyes to his, there was a resolution in her face he'd never seen before. "It's time, Charlie. You had a good run. Three decades." She shook her head. "But no more. You need to let it go."

Panic crowded in around him and put its cold fingers against his throat. "I'm a bookseller, Donna." His voice was pinched, his heart pounding. "I don't know what else to do."

She shook her head, glancing about as if the answer might be somewhere on the barren walls. "You know retail." Pain colored her eyes. "Costco or one of the supermarkets. Someone has to be hiring."

Charlie shuddered at the picture. He was almost sixty, his hair whiter than the snow outside. Pushing carts at Costco? Bagging groceries at Kroger? How could that be his swan song when he had planned to work at The Bridge until God took him home? He gave her a weak smile. "I'll figure something out."

"You have to close the store. We can't afford the lease." Her eyebrows raised, she studied him, searching his intentions. "You know that. Right?"

He couldn't have felt more pressure if the roof collapsed and pinned him to the floor. Sweat beaded on his forehead, and he wiped it with the back of his hands. He felt a hundred years old. "I have to do something. I know that."

A long pause followed while she watched him. "I'm going home." She held her hand out. "Come with me?"

"Not yet." He shook his head, and again panic breathed its icy breath down his back. The store *was* his home, his family. Leaving it now without an answer was like putting his mother out in the cold and wishing her the best of luck. He couldn't do it, couldn't promise anything other than the obvious. "I have to think."

A tired sigh sounded in her throat and she put her hand alongside his face. "I love you, Charlie. It's not your fault. Bookstores everywhere are dealing with this." She smiled at him. "I believe in you."

"I know." He gave her a brave smile and a look that said he'd be fine, that she could go and he would find the answers somehow. The truth was, Donna didn't understand completely. This wasn't any other bookstore. It was Franklin's bookstore. A place that defined downtown. If people knew he was in trouble, they'd help, right? They'd come together and do whatever it took to save The Bridge.

Donna kissed him good-bye, pulled up the hood of her winter coat, and headed out into the cold. When he was alone again, Charlie thought about the town coming together. He walked slowly to the window and watched Donna hurry around the corner, out of sight. On both sides of the street, people were walking and laughing and drifting in and out of the small boutiques along the avenue, shopping bags draped on their arms.

Who was he kidding?

People rallying around a bookstore? Things like that only happened in the movies. If The Bridge closed, people wouldn't notice. They would move on and find their books somewhere else, same as any other city in America that lost a bookstore this year. They'd jump on Amazon or get a Kindle for Christmas, and Franklin would go on as if nothing had happened. And that would be that. Charlie Barton and The Bridge, and every memory of anything wonderful that happened here, forever drowned in the flood.

He moved back from the window and shuffled to the checkout counter. The structure was built-in, so it had withstood the rains, and with it, the one item he intended to save. He opened the swollen top drawer and carefully, gingerly, pulled out the scrapbook. Water had risen past the counter and the drawers, but somehow, the scrapbook wasn't destroyed. He ran his hand over the stained canvas cover and the blurred image of The Bridge, the way it had looked in 1972—when Charlie first leased the old house and opened the shop.

The picture on the front of the book was unrecognizable, but between the covers, the photographs remained remarkably unscathed. Charlie opened it and lingered on the first spread. The scrapbook was from a widow named Edna Carlton who had lost her husband in the Vietnam War. In her loneliness and grief, Edna had found her way to The Bridge. "The books, the coffee, the conversation, all of it has been wonderful," she had written across the top of the first page.

"The Bridge has given me a second chance at life. Fill this book with the stories of old souls like me. People who sometimes need a place like this to bridge yesterday and tomorrow. People looking for a second chance. Thank you, Charlie."

Below the inscription, a photo showed Edna Carlton sitting demurely in the upright chair that once stood at the far corner of the store. She held a used copy of *Little Women* in her hands, a story that helped her get through her husband's death. Charlie couldn't read the title of the book. The picture wasn't that clear. Quite simply, he remembered Edna and the book that had spoken so deeply to her.

The way he remembered all of them, generations of regulars who had found a home away from home at The Bridge.

With great reverence, he thumbed through the book, stopping at the photo of the businesswoman Matilda Owens, who had used The Bridge to study for her law degree in the nineties. Last Charlie heard, Matilda had made partner at a law firm off Michigan Avenue in Chicago. Next were a banker and his wife, who had used The Bridge as a romantic hideaway where they often read to each other. Charlie could picture them, whispering beautiful passages from *Wuthering Heights,* together at the end of the old worn sofa that used to sit near The Bridge's fireplace, finding their way back to the feelings that marked the start of their own love story.

Charlie worked his way to the end of the scrapbook and stopped cold, his heart heavier than before. On the last page were two of his favorite people, a couple of college kids who had hung out at The Bridge for most of two years. He ran his thumb along the edge of the photo. Saddest day ever when he heard they separated. He used to tell Donna that the two of them were what love should look like.

Molly Evans and Ryan Kelly.

They had signed their names beneath the photo, but Charlie would've remembered them anyway. Ryan stopped in every once in a while when he was in town. Charlie would ask how he was doing, but they'd lost touch enough over the years that the conversation was never very deep. As far as Charlie knew, Ryan was playing music for a country band. All grown up and famous. Charlie wasn't sure if he ever married. Usually he talked more about Charlie than himself.

Molly hadn't been around since she left town after

her sophomore year. Married some guy on the West Coast, according to Ryan. Such a shame. The two of them should've found a way to stay together. Their differences couldn't have compared to the way the two of them shone so brightly together. Even now Charlie believed that if The Bridge were still standing, still in business, one day Molly would come back. His customers always found a way back.

But not if he closed his doors.

He shut the scrapbook and slipped it carefully back into the drawer. Then he leaned against the wall and breathed in deep. The place smelled dank and moldy. He had plans to paint the walls and bring in new carpet, improvements that would remove the odor. The line of credit was supposed to pay for that, too.

Father, what am I supposed to do? There has to be an answer. My dad said this would happen, and I never believed it, so You can't let me fail. Please, God...

He turned and faced the wall, spread his hands against the cool bricks. The Union soldiers had felt warm and safe and dry here, as if things might turn out okay after all. He squeezed his eyes shut, his hands, his arms trembling from the great sorrow crushing in around him. *That's all I want, Lord... I'm begging You. Let me rebuild The Bridge so the flood doesn't win. Give me the second chance Edna talked about. Please, Lord, show me how.*

A Scripture passage whispered in his mind, one he'd shared with customers on occasion. It was from Deuteronomy 20:1: *When you go to war against your enemies and see horses and chariots and an army greater than yours, do not be afraid of them, because the Lord your God, who brought you up out of Egypt, will be with you.*

God had brought him out of Egypt, for sure, he and Donna both. Their own personal Egypt. A tragedy no one in Franklin knew anything about.

That horrific time had led them to move here, to open The Bridge and find solace in books. It was the only thing Charlie could think of that might bring meaning to his life after what had happened. Painful memories tried to work their way to the forefront of his heart, but he refused them, refused to go back. He had the photos, the newspaper clippings, tucked in a small metal box in the drawer beside the scrapbook. He never opened it, never looked back.

God had rescued them from that, Charlie had been completely convinced.

Now he wasn't so sure.

Fear and panic stood on either side of him as he turned and faced the front of his store. He had one more shot, one more chance at finding a loan. The banker and his wife—longtime customers—lived in town. The banker ran the branch in Cool Springs. Charlie hadn't wanted to borrow from someone he knew, but he had no choice. He would call in the morning and explain the situation. Then he would know for sure whether God was still with him.

Or if He, too, had left Charlie Barton with the floodwater.

CHAPTER THREE

Donna Barton couldn't stop crying.

All her life she'd counted on Charlie. She relied on him and looked up to him, and from their first date, she'd come to expect his smile and optimism. Even at their lowest point as a couple, Charlie had been rock-solid. Unsinkable. His faith in God strong enough to keep them standing, whatever threatened to topple them. Even death couldn't defeat Charlie Barton.

Until now.

Quiet sobs shook Donna's thin shoulders as she drove south from Franklin to their small ranch house just outside town. She had held it together at the store, but she'd never seen Charlie this way, afraid and without answers. As she left her husband behind, as she stepped into the uncertainty of whatever came next, the sidewalk beneath her feet felt like liquid and her mind raced with uncertainty. Noises around her faded until her senses filled with the sound of her heartbeat. For a moment she wondered if she were having a heart attack or a nervous breakdown. She stopped, grabbed hold of a light post, and prayed. Begged God for the strength to take the next step.

Somehow she'd gotten to her car.

The look in Charlie's eyes, his desperate tone, all of it stayed with her as she gripped the steering wheel. Could she have said anything different, anything that might've encouraged him? Her responses had been honest—The Bridge made a difference in Franklin and to the people who loved it. But that time was past. If they couldn't get a line of credit, then God was closing the bookstore, whether Charlie was ready or not. She had told him how she felt at the core of her existence.

She believed in him. She did.

But her belief in Charlie Barton wouldn't pay the bills or make the lease payment. That would happen only if Charlie picked himself up, headed down to Publix, and found a job. A way to keep them afloat. Maybe that's what scared her the most. She and Charlie didn't see the situation the same way. He wasn't ready to give up, and she loved that about him. Loved that he wasn't a quitter. But at this rate, they were going to lose more than the store. They were going to lose their house. Maybe she'd have to get a job, too. She could do that, right? Either way, Charlie needed to be realistic about the bookstore. She blinked back another rush of tears. Sometimes the only way to fight through a situation was to walk.

Give up one dream and take hold of another.

Donna settled back into her seat and tried to draw a full breath. The trouble had happened so suddenly. Neither of them had seen the flood coming, the flood that God could've prevented. Donna wiped her fingers beneath her eyes and tried to see the road ahead of her.

Snow like this hadn't fallen in November as far back as Donna could remember. Franklin didn't usually have temperatures below freezing until after Christmas, and the cold weather produced mostly flurries. Today two inches were forecast, with another five expected later in the week. By the looks of the snow coming down, the estimates were low. The sun had set hours ago, so Donna was mindful of ice on the road. She turned on the windshield wipers and squinted to see through the thickly falling snow.

Driving took enough of her attention that her tears slowed. The storm drew her back, took her to the place in Charlotte, North Carolina, where she and Charlie had met. Charlie, that handsome, strapping young man with calloused hands and a tender heart. The first person Donna ever trusted.

Her past remained as ugly as it was painful, but while she drove home, she could do nothing to stop it from replaying. Donna was the only child of drug-addicted parents, a bright girl who spent her teenage years visiting one or both of her parents in jail. Routinely, she would come home to find her mom and dad crashed on the floor, Ziploc bags of drugs and dirty needles scattered on the kitchen table.

Sometimes Donna spent the night with a friend down the street. Mostly, she took all her heartache and sorrow out on her studies. Along the way, she developed a fierce determination to succeed, to stay away from drugs and danger and anything that would distract her from her dream. She hid the truth about her home life from everyone and easily carried a perfect 4.0 through high school, and no one was surprised when Donna was named class valedictorian or when she earned a full-ride scholarship to North Carolina State.

Her mom overdosed on heroin three days before her graduation.

A teacher and her husband took Donna in, and she lived with them until she headed off for college. Her dad didn't handle the loss as well. He stayed around for a month or so and then one night went out with his friends and never came home. Police found his car wrapped around a tree the next morning. And like that, Donna was alone in the world.

By the time Donna met Charlie, she was utterly independent. People had let her down and hurt her, so if she could rely on herself, on her academic abilities and her dreams of teaching, then she would survive. Charlie was interesting and different. He was in her freshman English composition class, and from the first day, he found a way to make her laugh. He was the only son of a local cement contractor, a man gruff and quick-tempered who expected Charlie to take over the family trade. Charlie didn't want to spend his life leveling fresh-poured foundations and patios. His decision to study business at NC State was the most rebellious thing he had ever done, and it created a rift with his parents that remained.

Donna remembered what Charlie's father had told him, and the memories made her sick to her stomach. *You'll never succeed in the business world,* his father had told him. *You're a Barton, and Bartons aren't businesspeople. You'll fail and then you'll come crawling back to me and the cement.*

Though his father had sold the cement business fifteen years ago, Charlie was still desperate to hang on to the bookstore. If he walked away from The Bridge now, his father would be right. Donna felt fresh tears fill her eyes. The enormity of that awful prediction must have weighed heavy on Charlie's heart.

"Really, God? You'd let this happen to a man like Charlie?" She whispered the words, her voice broken.

She squinted again, the moments of her past still playing in her mind. No one had ever been able to reach her like Charlie Barton had. When the semester ended, Charlie took her to the beach and walked with her along the shore. "Look out there, Donna." He stopped and stared out at the water, a smile filling his face. "What do you see?"

She laughed, nervous and excited and feeling more alive than ever. "Everything and nothing. I can't see the end of it."

"Exactly." He turned and faced her, touching her cheek with his fingertips. "That's what you deserve, Donna. Everything in all the world. Without end."

"Is that right?" She had felt herself blush, felt the unfamiliarity of caring and wanting and longing for someone. "What if you're the only one who thinks so?"

His smile made her feel dizzy. A sparkle shone in his eyes, and he shrugged. "Then I guess it'll be up to me to make sure you get what you deserve."

Somewhere between his sweet declaration and the walk back to the car, Donna remembered taking note of two things: the feel of the wind and sun on her shoulders and something else. Something was missing from her chest, and she realized by the time they were in his car that it was her heart.

Because from that day on, her heart belonged always and only to Charlie Barton.

Their wedding two years later was a simple affair in front of a justice of the peace, followed by their honeymoon, a weekend trip to a friend's lakeside cabin.

After that, they shared a small apartment, and at night when they had no money, they would sit across from each other at their small kitchen table and dream. One conversation from those days stood out—Donna could see it, hear it as if watching a movie.

"My dad never let me read." Charlie reached across the table and took her hands in his.

"What?" She gave him a doubtful look. "Be serious."

He raised one eyebrow and tilted his head. His sad chuckle told her he wasn't kidding. "I mean, in my early school years, he wanted me to read textbooks. Never for fun." He ran his thumbs along the sides of her hands. "But I loved reading."

Donna smiled. "Me, too."

Charlie told her how, in middle school, he'd head to the school library instead of going outside at recess. "I fought alongside Jim Hawkins in *Treasure Island,* and I felt the splash of water on my face as I sailed on muddy rivers with Tom Sawyer." He laughed. "I was probably the only guy in eighth grade who cried when Beth died in *Little Women.*"

Charlie's fascination with fiction led him to check out books and sneak them home in his schoolbag.

He'd hide whatever he was reading beneath his bed, and long after his dad thought he was asleep, he'd slip under the covers and read by flashlight.

"So I was thinking," he told her early in their marriage, "maybe I'll open a bookstore. New and used books—so everyone has a chance to see the world through the pages of a story."

Donna had been delighted at the idea, impressed with her larger-than-life husband and his grand dreams. His heart had always been bigger than the ocean she'd looked across on that long-ago day. Opening a bookstore had never been about making a fortune or finding the quickest way to success. He simply wanted other people to experience what he had experienced. The feel of ocean water on their feet as they salvaged a shipwreck next to Robinson Crusoe.

Neither of them expected Donna to get pregnant six months into their marriage. They had school to finish and the bookstore to build after that. Even then, Charlie was undaunted.

"God's unexpected blessing," he would say. "He must have mighty plans for this little one."

Donna blinked back the memory. What happened

next was the hardest part, the piece of their past that Donna rarely allowed to surface. Her pregnancy was healthy, nothing out of the ordinary until she went into labor. She had no idea why it had happened or why hers was the one pregnancy in tens of thousands that ended the way it did. There were no warnings, no signs that an emergency was at hand.

One morning a week from her due date, she woke up bleeding.

Charlie rushed her to the hospital, but Donna was already in and out of consciousness. *Losing a lot of blood . . . DIC . . . placenta previa . . . coagulation . . .* Unfamiliar words and terms were thrown around by the doctor and nursing staff as they worked in a panic around her. The last thing she saw before she passed out was Charlie, his wide eyes and pale face as someone asked him to leave the room.

Then there was nothing but darkness.

When Donna woke up, she felt like she'd been run over. Charlie was at her side, tears in his eyes. A hundred questions screamed through her mind, but she didn't need to ask any of them. The pain in her sweet husband's face told her all the sad answers without him saying a word. Eventually, when he could talk, he looked her straight in the eyes and gave her the truth. The baby was dead, a little girl.

That wasn't all. Donna's bleeding had been so bad that the doctor had performed a hysterectomy to save her life. So Donna's chances to ever get pregnant again were dead, too.

In time her body healed, but her heart, her soul, never would have recovered without Charlie. If he questioned God for allowing their loss, he never said so. He clipped their daughter's tiny obituary from the newspaper and placed it with her hospital bracelet and her death certificate in a small metal box. Proof that she had existed. Other than his tears on that first day, he remained solid, convincing her day by day that he loved her unconditionally. Never mind the babies she could never give him. He loved her.

Completely and wholeheartedly.

———

Donna wiped her eyes again and pulled into their driveway. The gravel was slick, covered with a layer of snow. She hoped Charlie was behind her, that he hadn't stayed at the store looking for answers that weren't there. As she parked the car and made her way into the house through the driving snow, she felt the familiar fear again. *Dear God . . . don't let anything happen to him . . . I've never seen him like this . . .*

She made herself a cup of tea and took the seat by the window so she could watch for him. Again the memories returned. It was Charlie's idea that they leave North Carolina and start life over again in Franklin. He had heard from one of his professors that investors were eyeing the small town south of Nashville and that the place was expected to become a retreat for Music City's elite and a destination for tourists.

"The perfect place for our bookstore." Charlie's enthusiasm was contagious, and at the end of the semester, one of his professors connected him with a friend in Nashville who had a room for rent. Charlie was relentless in pursuit of his dream.

They lived in a garage apartment behind the friend's house, and Charlie worked three jobs while attending school so he could save money for the bookstore. Two years after graduation, Donna took a job teaching at Franklin Elementary School, and Charlie leased space for the store.

He called it The Bridge because that was how he felt about books. They connected the past and the present, the present and the future. Books brought people together and gave them a path to worlds they wouldn't otherwise experience.

There was another reason, too.

The bookstore wasn't only Charlie's dream. It was the way to move from the pain of the past to the promise of tomorrow. Forever there would be the tragic and disappointing life before opening the store and the hopeful, fulfilling life after. The store wasn't only called The Bridge.

It *was* the bridge.

From the beginning, Charlie was too generous to make much of a profit. A college kid would come in looking for a classic and end up being a dollar or two short. "Don't worry about it. Someday someone will need a favor from you." Charlie would wink at him and tuck the book in a bag. "Be ready for that moment."

When illness struck the owner of a neighboring pastry business, Charlie gathered up a week's worth of receipts, took the cash to the little shop, and laid it on the counter. "We have to stick together. Community's more important than making a killing."

Donna remembered the woman who owned the pastry shop telling her about Charlie's statement. Donna had laughed out loud. "Sweet Charlie." Her heart swelled at her husband's kindness. "He would give it all away long before there was any danger of making a killing."

That stayed true year after year, decade after decade, while the people of Franklin and tourists who passed through found respite and adventure, hope and direction at The Bridge. Through it all, Charlie never questioned God about the losses of the past, about her parents' drug addiction, or his father's decision to cut him out of the family.

Or about the loss of their little girl.

Even when the flood took every book in the store, Donna didn't see Charlie waver, didn't see him fear for the future. Not until today, when hope of opening again was finally and fully dead. Donna sipped her tea and prayed, begging God on behalf of her husband. Instead of feeling peace and certainty, the more Donna cried out to God, the more she became filled with a sense of dread. If The Bridge closed, then the predictions of Charlie's father would come true. No matter what good Charlie had done at The Bridge, he would be left with the one lie big enough to destroy him.

The lie that somehow Charlie Barton had failed.

CHAPTER FOUR

Music had changed, that was the problem.

Ryan Kelly was a guitar player, and players always had work in Nashville. Now, though, a glut of musicians and too many lesser-known acts had dropped the price for a day's work. Ryan wasn't sure he could still make a living at it.

He silenced his alarm clock, stepped out of bed in his Nashville apartment, and raked his hand through his messy dark hair. How had things changed so fast? A month ago he was touring with a group that used to be the nation's hottest country duo. Now he was unemployed and ready to head back to Carthage, Mississippi.

The past five years were little more than a blur. After graduation from Belmont, he was hired to play with an unknown country act. The pair wound up winning big at the Country Music Awards a year later, and Ryan was set: the lead guitarist for an act that had toured as many as two hundred days a year over the last five years.

But music was a fickle master, and three straight records without a hit were more than the label could take. When the group got dropped over the summer, the lead singer asked Ryan to stay with them through the end of the touring season. Now it was the Saturday after Thanksgiving, and he'd been home a full week without any idea of what was coming next.

He stood and walked to his bedroom window. Crazy snowstorm wouldn't let up. It made him wonder if he was really in Nashville, or maybe some other city, ready to hit the stage. As if all of the past week had been a terrible dream.

He narrowed his eyes against the blinding white outside. *Where do You want me, God? What am I supposed to do next?* He stared at his alarm clock. Seven in the morning. All his life he'd set an alarm—something his father had taught him. "Successful people get up first thing in the morning." His hardworking dad lived out the truth, teaching in the Carthage school system for going on three decades. "Don't get in the habit of sleeping late."

Ryan leaned back against the windowsill. His room was clean, laundry caught up, and every inch of the house dusted and tidied. Getting things in order was the way he always spent the first few days after a tour. This time was different, his alarm only one more reminder of the reality: He had no next tour to prepare for, nothing ahead but the days.

Ryan breathed in deep. How strange that the changes in music hadn't touched him until now.

"It's a new world," his booking agent had told him. The man was a twenty-year veteran in country music. "Players are making a fifth of what they once did. The money's in songwriting and studio work."

"Bands still need guitarists." Ryan hadn't wanted to believe it. He'd assumed for the last six months that when the tour ran out, he'd come home, make a few phone calls, and hook up with a new band.

"It's not that simple." His agent sighed. "The successful acts make their players part of the group. Otherwise it's petty cash for a night's play. Even studio work is different. More competitive than I've seen it. A lot of producers use computerized instruments."

In the dozens of phone calls he'd made over the last week, Ryan had learned of just one job opening.

Studio work for one of the labels, a job coming up the first week of December. His agent said the studio expected more than a hundred players to show up and vie for the job. Ryan breathed in deep and headed toward his bathroom.

There was one other option.

His father had told him about it last night. The music teacher position at Carthage High was opening up at the end of the semester—six months earlier than expected. "It's a good job," his dad told him, "safe, secure."

He thanked his father, but when he hung up, he could only think about the reason he'd gone after his dream of playing guitar professionally in the first place, the reason that, after graduation, he hadn't been able to go back to Kristen and her father's farm and the two acres set aside for them. The reason he had stayed in Nashville nearly a year after graduation, taking odd jobs until he got his shot.

Because even now he could hear her voice encouraging him, pushing him. The voice of Molly Allen. The girl he hadn't been able to forget no matter how hard he tried, no matter how many years.

He showered and dressed in worn dark jeans and

an off-white thermal. Like every day, today offered
another chance. He could go to the label and talk to
one of the execs, see if he'd missed something—a new
band or one of the regulars looking for a replacement.
He could be part of a group, right? Throughout his
morning routine, while he combed his hair and
brushed his teeth, while he made the decision about
heading down to the label's office, Ryan thought about
her.

About Molly.

Where was she after all these years? Still in San
Francisco, married to the guy her parents had chosen
for her? Ryan had heard that from someone, and the
truth hurt. Not because she'd gone back home or because she'd never fallen for him despite their friendship. But because she'd broken her promise.

The promise to never settle.

Ryan scrambled four eggs and dished them onto a
plate. As he did, his eyes fell on the bookcase just off
the dining room. The book had been there for the
past seven years, but today it might as well have had a
neon sign over it. His copy of *Jane Eyre*. He looked at
it for a long time before he pushed his plate back,
stood, and crossed the room. When he reached the

bookcase, he stared at it, unable to fight the way the physical presence of the book took him back.

Molly had bought a copy for each of them one of the last times they were together. "We won't be here to read it off the shelf," Molly had told him. "So we both need a copy."

By then their good-bye loomed, and her voice was tinged with tears. Somehow she had believed that if they each had a copy of *Jane Eyre*, they would keep the connection they'd found at The Bridge. He pulled the book from the shelf and held it carefully, as if it were the most priceless heirloom. His copy was used, one of the earlier editions. Molly had special-ordered it through Charlie once she knew for sure she was leaving.

He opened the worn cover and stared at the inscription. *I would do anything for you, sir. Anything that was right . . . Love, Molly.*

Anything that was right. The line from the novel had stayed with him, haunting him daily at first. How could she have thought that the most right thing was to leave, to find her way back to a life her parents had planned for her? And how could she have married Preston Millington when she had never loved the guy?

Not until two years later had he picked up the book and read through it. He was on the road then, but between shows on the bus, in the quiet of his bunk, he journeyed once more through the story of Jane Eyre. Only then did he see what Molly had written at the back of the book. Another quote from the novel's protagonist, but one that held an insight he didn't quite understand.

Her inscription was this: *All has changed, sir. I must leave you.*

"What changed, Molly?" He whispered the question, as confused today as he was back then. He held the book to his chest and leaned his shoulder against the bookcase. The snow falling out the front window took him back, and gradually, the images around him faded until all he could see was yesterday.

Seven years of yesterdays ago.

———

That day the staff at Molly's house was off—at least that was the plan. Ryan and Molly had reached the end of their second year at Belmont, and finals were a few weeks away. The idea of sharing dinner at the big house in Brentwood was Molly's idea. "I'll make pasta primavera," she told him. Her eyes danced at the thought. "My dad will never find out." She hesitated, and her face lit up. "Actually, come early and we'll work together."

They skipped The Bridge that day. After school they went to the market and bought a cartful of groceries, laughing all the while at how two people could eat so much food. As close as they'd been, Molly had never brought him to her house for fear of her father. Not until they walked through her front door with two bags each did Ryan fully grasp the wealth she came from. The house was a mansion decorated with the sort of furnishings and artwork Ryan had never seen outside magazines and TV shows.

"What's your house in San Francisco look like?" He put his hands in his pockets and cast her a bewildered look.

She grinned and gave a slight roll of her eyes. "You don't want to know."

Ryan had a feeling she was right. "I bet my parents' house would fit in your garage."

"Yeah." She made a face that showed she was uncomfortable with the conversation. "Let's talk about something else."

"Like how come we're starting the primavera sauce with a pile of vegetables." He came over and nudged her with his elbow. "Mine always comes from a jar."

"Yours?" Her eyes sparkled. "Come on, Ryan. Don't tell me you've made pasta primavera before."

"Hmm." He leaned against the kitchen counter and studied her. "Does spaghetti sauce count?"

"No." She washed her hands, her eyes on him the whole time. "True primavera sauce starts with a soffritto of garlic and olive oil."

"Soffritto?" Ryan couldn't say the word without laughing. "You didn't tell me you were a culinary expert."

"I'm not." She dried her hands and pulled two cutting boards from beneath an eight-burner stove. "Just because I can order it off a menu doesn't mean I can make it." She grinned. "You're my guinea pig."

"Oh, is that right?"

"Yes." She laughed and handed him a bag of broccoli. "Start cutting. Let's see what we come up with."

Somewhere between chopping broccoli and sautéing the soffritto, Ryan felt the mood between them change. Molly had turned his head from the first time he saw her, but she was off-limits. Practically engaged to the guy back home. And he had Kristen waiting for him in Carthage. But that night in the kitchen of her enormous Brentwood home, there was only the two of them. Way before they sat down to eat, Ryan felt a sense of inevitability about what was coming. As if they were no longer two college friends aware of their limitations, but characters from some classic love story.

They didn't talk about it, didn't make commentary on the emotions flying between them. They simply lived in the moment. When dinner was over, she turned on music and took him outside. The house backed up to a forest, but the yard sat beneath open skies, and that night the host of stars seemed hung for them alone. She led him to the backside of a gorgeous swimming pool where they sat in a cushioned glider. Usually, at The Bridge, they kept distance between them, enough so they could turn and face each other and read from *Jane Eyre* or compare notes from their various classes.

That night they sat with their bodies touching, and Ryan wondered if she felt it, too. The electricity between them, as if all their lives had led to this. The air was warm, and they wore T-shirts and shorts. As they set the glider in gentle motion, every whisper of her bare arm against his, every touch of their knees, every rapid beat of his anxious heart, made him wonder how long he could wait. Because with everything in him, he wanted to kiss her.

He found a resolve he hadn't known he was capable of and forced himself to look up at the stars. "So beautiful." He was talking about her, but he couldn't let on. Who was he kidding? The feelings between them were impossible, right? She hadn't come to Belmont to fall in love. And even though he and Kristen hadn't talked in over a week, he would have to end things with her before he could think about Molly the way he was thinking about her there in the glider.

A comfortable silence settled around them, and finally, Molly sighed, her eyes still on the sky. "My dad isn't sure about me finishing up here. He wants me to come home."

Fear breathed icy cold down the back of Ryan's neck. "What?" He kept his tone in check. "Why would he do that? You're halfway finished."

Though she laughed, the sound was desperately

sad. "He doesn't care about my music. He wants me to sit at the head of his empire one day." She gave him a weak smile. "I'm the son he never had. That's what he always tells me."

"Molly." He eased away and turned to face her. "You haven't taken a single business class."

"It doesn't matter." She didn't laugh. "He'll have me surrounded by experts. He wants our family to maintain control." She took a slow breath. "He says I'll learn on the job."

"You're only twenty." Ryan couldn't believe the man was serious. "He wouldn't put you in that position now."

"No." She managed a light bit of laughter at the idea. "He wants to groom me, have me finish classes closer to his headquarters, take me to the meetings, and get me familiar with operations. Grooming is like, I don't know, a ten-year process."

It felt like a prison sentence, but Ryan didn't say so. He slid back to his spot beside her and set the glider in motion.

"You think I'm giving up." She sounded hurt, and this time she shifted so she could see him. "That's why you're not saying anything?"

He stopped the glider and met her eyes. "You're the one with a dream, right? Playing in the philharmonic?"

"What can I do about it?" Her tone flashed a rare anger. "My whole life has led to this. I've known what I was supposed to do, where I was supposed to live, since . . . since the first grade."

"He can't make you." Ryan stood and walked to the edge of the patio. For a long time he stayed there, staring into the forest, trying to see clear of the heartache ahead if she left. Suddenly, the reasons seemed clear and he spun around, his own voice louder than before. "It's safe. That's what this is about. You could tell him no, Molly." He was breathing hard, his emotions getting ahead of him. "But going home and doing what he says is safer."

For a few seconds, it looked like she might refute him. Instead, moving slowly, she came to him, and the anger between them kindled a passion they had denied from the beginning. She stood inches from him, her body trembling, and when she spoke, her voice was a whisper. "I hate safe." She came closer still, and tears filled her eyes. "I want to be like Jane Eyre." She sniffed, her voice breaking. "'I am no bird; and no net ensnares me: I am a free human being with an independent will.'" She let her forehead fall against his chest. "Help me, Ryan. Please. Help me be free."

He felt his head spinning, his heart pounding. He took a half step back so he could think clearly, her quote from *Jane Eyre* still playing in his mind. No matter how he fought for control, his voice betrayed the depth of his feelings for her. "How, Molly? How can I help?"

She didn't hesitate and suddenly he could see her again, feel her breath against his skin that summer night. She closed the distance between them once more, and with a determination and anguish that made her breathtakingly beautiful, she took his face in her hands. "Kiss me. Give me a reason to stay."

Here was the moment he had hoped for and dreamed of and wondered about. Though everything about it was wrong, Ryan couldn't stop himself. He caught the back of her head in his hands and slowly, in a losing battle of restraint, he drew her to him and touched his lips to hers. The kiss was more magical than anything in a book. And for the next minute he was convinced for the first time that he wasn't the only one who'd been fighting the attraction. Their kiss grew and built until they were breathless, and then, as if she remembered all the reasons they shouldn't be together, she put her hands on his shoulders and drew back from him. "Ryan . . . we can't."

"Hey . . ." He tried to see into her eyes, but she was staring at the ground, shame covering her face. "Don't be afraid. You said you hate safe, remember?"

"No." When she looked up, the questions in her heart seemed to scream for answers. "You have Kristen. This is . . . it's wrong."

He wanted to remind her that the idea of kissing had been hers, but he was dizzy from the feel of her in his arms, from her lips against his. "I'm sorry." It was the only thing he knew to say. She was right. Until he broke things off with his long-distance high school sweetheart, he had no business kissing Molly Allen. For now, though, if this was what it took to convince her to stay at Belmont, he wasn't really sorry at all. "I'm really sorry, Molly."

"Are you?" She was still breathing fast, as caught up in the wanting and fighting their forbidden attraction as he was. "Are you sorry about this?"

His answer didn't come in words. He took her again in his arms and kissed her the way he had always wanted to kiss her. With all the romance of a character from one of their favorite books. He still wondered what would've happened next, how far things might have gone. But a few minutes later, he caught someone moving in the upstairs window at the back of her house.

"The staff." He gasped the words and moved quickly away from her. "Molly." He nodded toward the window. "You said they were out for the night."

She followed his gaze, and as she did, they watched a light turn off inside the house. Fear flashed like lightning across Molly's face. "Do you think they saw us?"

"I'm not sure." He wanted to say who cared what the staff saw, wanted to draw her close again and pick up where they'd left off. But he respected her too much for that. "Would they tell your dad?"

"Definitely." She glanced around, clearly searching for a way out. "You need to leave." Her eyes pleaded with him to understand. "I can't give my parents another reason to send me home."

For a long moment he hesitated. Did it really matter what her parents thought or what her father threatened? She was old enough to make her own decisions. Ryan felt frustrated to the depths of his being. He could only try to understood a little of Molly's pressures. She'd answered to her father all her life— that much was obvious. But if he knew Molly at all, someday she would find a way to stand on her own. Even if, for now, her determination to please her father overpowered her own dreams.

Ryan blinked, the memory of her kiss lodged in some locked-up corner of his heart. Always when he looked back, he could peg that backyard embrace to the beginning of the end. He put the book back on the shelf, face out. Jane never knew what would happen next. So the only change Molly could've been refer- ring to at the back of his copy had to be the one he couldn't refute.

The change in her heart.

CHAPTER FIVE

That night after their kiss Molly hurried him to the side gate. In the shadows he hugged her, holding on as long as he could. "You said to give you a reason." He touched her cheek, feeling the urgency of the situation. "Give me time, Molly. Don't leave."

A quick nod, and she checked over his shoulder. "We'll talk tomorrow. At The Bridge."

But the next day, before classes, Ryan's cell phone rang. The memory of the phone call still made his stomach hurt. The man was gruff from the beginning. "Is this Ryan Kelly?"

"Yes." It wasn't quite seven in the morning, and Ryan had been rushing around his room gathering homework for class. He stopped and stared at the phone. The caller ID was blocked. "Who's this?"

"Wade Allen. I'm Molly's father." He sounded disgusted. "Look, I know about last night."

Ryan stopped short. "What?" Was this really happening? Molly's father calling him? Why would the man be awake at this hour? "How'd you get my number?"

"That's none of your business." He barely paused. His voice was clipped and pronounced, the talk of an agitated and highly educated man. "Look, I know you have feelings for my daughter. But I'd like to ask you, man to man, to think about Molly and not yourself."

"You don't know her." Sudden venom spewed from Ryan's voice. How dare her father do this, call and try to manipulate him. "She doesn't want to work for you."

"Listen to me, young man. *You* don't know her." His voice maintained a chilling level of calm. "Molly is in love with Preston Millington." A dramatic pause filled the line. "They're engaged to be married."

Slowly, Ryan dropped to the edge of his twin bed. He pressed his elbows into his knees and tried to catch his breath. "She's not engaged. She would've told me."

"They've set a wedding date. Two years from this

summer." He laughed, but the sound came across as condescending. "Molly is very young. This whole Belmont thing was her way of being sure about the engagement."

Hope breathed the slightest air into his lungs. "Have you talked to her lately, sir? She's not sure. I can promise you that."

"She's sure." His answer was quick. "She called Preston yesterday afternoon and told him she was coming home in a few weeks. When she finishes final exams." He sighed as if he could barely be bothered with the conversation. "I'm asking you to stay out of her life. Don't confuse her. She knows what she wants, and she knows where she belongs." This time his quiet laughter mocked Ryan in every way possible. "A guy like you? From Carthage, Mississippi? You could never give her the life she's accustomed to." He chuckled. "You didn't actually *believe* she'd fall for you."

"What if she already has?" Ryan had no trouble standing up to him. "You can't control her."

"I didn't want to have to do this."

"You're not going to do anything. Molly's entitled to live her life, to follow her dreams and—"

"Look." His tone was sharp again, the laughter gone. "Don't believe me. Let her tell you." There was a clicking sound, and what could only have been a recording of Molly's voice. She sounded upset. "Yes, Preston . . . you know how I feel about you. I've known you all my life. I told you I wouldn't stay at Belmont forever." Another clicking sound, and when her father spoke again, satisfaction rang in his tone. "Did you hear that? And yes, I recorded her." He sounded defensive. "She called Preston here at the office. I'm a powerful businessman. I record all my conversations!" He took a breath and seemed to steady himself. "I'm letting you listen to it because I want you to know the truth."

Ryan's head was spinning. He couldn't find the words to speak.

"Look, kid. You heard her. She's in love with Preston, and she's coming home." His words were like so many bullets, steady and well aimed. "If you care about her, you'll cut things off quickly. Let her go. Anything else will only confuse her."

Ryan felt himself drowning, gasping for a way to keep his head above water. There was none. The voice was hers, the message clearly her side of a conversation with the guy waiting for her in San Francisco. Ryan wanted to shout at the man. There had to be an explanation. Molly wasn't in love with Preston. If she were, she would've said so. Shock quickly became fury against her father, rage that rose up and consumed him. He didn't say another word. He ended the call, tossed his phone on his pillow, and punched his fist. Punched it so hard his palm was bruised and swollen by the time he picked her up.

Their routine that day was the same, but their conversation was short and stilted. He had no intention of honoring her father's wishes, so he didn't dream of ending things. But the chemistry that had captured them the night before was gone, and Ryan knew why. With every passing hour, he had to admit the truth. He could be mad at Molly's father, but the voice was hers. Which could mean only one thing: Her father was telling the truth. Molly's true feelings were not for him but for Preston Millington.

When their classes were over that day, they drove to The Bridge, like always. This time when they found their spot upstairs, Ryan faced her. "Hey, listen. I'm sorry. About last night . . . I shouldn't have kissed you."

"What?" Her response was more of a quiet gasp.

"You've got your life back home." He smiled at her as if the words weren't killing him. "I have mine."

She shook her head. "Ryan, that's crazy." She raised her voice and then caught herself. "You told me to give you time. That you would show me why I shouldn't leave."

"I was wrong." He took a step back. With everything in him he forced himself not to think about how she had felt in his arms the night before. "We made a mistake, Molly. We're friends. Let's not let last night change that."

She looked like she might argue with him, but then she must've remembered Preston. A resignation came over her, and when she spoke again, he could see in her eyes walls around her heart that hadn't been there before. "You're right." Her smile looked forced. "I'm sorry, too." She shrugged. "Just one of those things, I guess."

Their study time went late, as usual. But nothing between them was ever the same again. Every time he saw her after that, he could only think of her conversation with Preston and the fact that when the semester ended, she was headed back. He felt like a blind fool. He must've been crazy to think he could win her heart or that she would walk away from her family for him. No matter what he wanted to believe, she was going home.

As the final days of the semester flew by, he and Molly found a way back to their friendship. He never told her about her father's phone call, never asked why she would promise her love to Preston that afternoon and then hours later lead Ryan to believe they were sharing the most wonderful night together. And he never asked her about their kiss, even though the questions plagued him every day. Hadn't they both felt the connection? Felt it to the core of their beings? How could she be so heartless, so conflicted? Every time he asked himself, the answers were the same. Which was why he never brought the matter up to Molly, even when he was tempted to ask. Clearly, she wasn't conflicted at all. She had pulled away from him after that night for one reason.

She was in love with Preston.

The memories lifted and Ryan stepped away from the window, from the snow falling outside. He needed to make calls, needed to check on the studio position. He wasn't ready to give up his dream. Not yet. Not the way Molly had given up when she left Belmont early that summer. Ryan hesitated and touched the copy of *Jane Eyre* as he passed by. He grabbed the keys to his truck and a heavy coat from the closet. Along the way, a thought occurred to him.

Of course he never said anything to Molly about her dad's phone call—not only because of Molly's taped conversation. But because she'd given up on the two of them so easily.

Three weeks later, when she announced she was headed back to San Francisco, there was no surprise, nothing he could say, no real argument or debate. They finished the semester and took their finals, and she bought them matching copies of *Jane Eyre*. Then she was gone. Leaving him with the one thought he couldn't get out of his mind. Her father might've been right about Molly's feelings for Preston. But if Molly truly believed Ryan wasn't good enough, the sad truth was this: He had never known Molly Allen at all.

───────

As on most Saturdays, Molly woke up just after six and climbed into her Nike running sweats, pale pink

and tight enough to keep out the cold on chilly November mornings like this. She had a routine that
took her down Twenty-third to Everett, up the hill to
the right, and through several smaller residential
streets back to her apartment. The route was four
miles, long enough to stir her heart and clear her
head.

At least on most Saturdays.

Today, as she set out, last night's video played in
her soul, the unanswered questions hanging from the
rafters of long ago. There had never been anyone like
Ryan, and Molly fully expected there never would be.
How had everything fallen apart? What could have
caused him to change so quickly?

There had been so much she wanted to say to him
before she returned home. But in the end, the only
thing she had done was ask him to kiss her. One kiss.
She jogged down her front steps and made the turn
onto Twenty-third, the wind biting against her cheeks.
The cold didn't matter. All she could feel were his
warm hands on her face, the strength of his arms. The
way she'd felt safe and loved and whole for those few
minutes.

This many years later, that single kiss, those

stolen moments in the backyard of her parents' Brentwood house, were the most romantic of her life. Her whole life. In his embrace, she felt herself falling, changing, finding the strength to stand up to her father. She had meant what she'd said to Ryan Kelly that night. All she needed was a reason—and he was her reason.

She was sure of that back then.

Even after they'd been caught, her only fear was her father, whether he'd find out and buy her a ticket home. Either the staff never saw the two of them kissing in the backyard or they never contacted her dad, because nothing was ever said. She didn't talk to her dad until a few weeks later, and by then she had her answer. She was going back home. Not because of his demands but because Ryan had changed his mind.

She knew something was wrong the moment he picked her up for school the next morning. Molly had planned out the moment. In her dreams, he would jump out and open the door for her—same as always—but when they were inside, he would draw her to him once more, and the kiss that had been cut short the night before would continue. It would continue and it would never end. Not ever.

Instead, Ryan was distant and cool. He opened her door, but he seemed careful not to let their arms brush. On the drive to Belmont, he said very little, talking only about the test he had that day in music theory and how he needed to buckle down and study more for his history class.

By this time Molly began to feel sick. It was almost as if someone had come in the still of the night and kidnapped the Ryan she had known, the best friend of two years who had made her believe he was falling for her. As if he had been replaced with someone who looked like him and dressed like him and smelled like him. Someone who drove his truck and attended his classes.

After that, the Ryan Kelly she knew no longer existed.

All day she worked up the courage to talk to him, to ask him what was wrong and demand that he be honest. But when they reached The Bridge a few hours later, he spoke before she had the chance. In a few rushed sentences, he apologized for the night before, calling it a mistake. He told her she had her life back home and he had his. She remembered wanting to scream at him or cry out or shake him. How many times had she told him she wasn't in love with Preston? Or that her dreams had nothing to do with running her father's corporation?

He was adamant, and in under a minute, the pieces came together. It wasn't her life back home that had caused him to rethink their night together, their kiss.

It was his.

He must have realized that in the end he would go back to Carthage and that he wasn't ready to break up with the girl waiting for him. He was still in love with her. That must have been the conclusion he had reached overnight, and now he could do nothing but apologize.

Molly shuddered, sickened by the thought as much now as she had been then. Could there be anything worse? The guy she'd spent two years with, so regretting kissing her that he had to apologize? In the same minute it had taken Molly to understand the reasons Ryan was sorry, she had known something else. She would never let him see her crumble. She wouldn't beg him or question him or convince him he was wrong. If he wouldn't let go of his past, she would do the only thing she had left.

She would go back home without him.

———

She told Ryan good-bye without tears, before she might've fallen apart. Between that and knowing with all certainty that she'd never see him again, Molly found a strength she hadn't thought herself capable of. It allowed her to go home and face her parents— something she hadn't been sure she could do.

The conversation with her father was short and to the point.

Her dad picked her up at the airport, and before they had her bags in the hired Town Car, he was telling her about meetings for the following day and the method of grooming and why it was important that she spend time watching him work so she'd know what was waiting for her ten years down the road.

Molly let him talk until they reached their gated home in Pacific Heights. When the driver let them out, she faced her father. "Stop."

". . . which is why we have two meetings tomorrow afternoon, the first with . . ." Her father blinked and seemed to register what she'd said. "Stop?"

"Yes." Her heart raced, but there was no turning back. "Here's how it will be. You need to know, because this is the last time I'm going to tell you."

He was quiet for the first time since Molly could remember.

"Okay." She smiled to cover up the fact that she was shaking. "I'm not ever going to be CEO of your corporation. But I have a deal for you."

Her dad looked like he might yell or fly into a dissertation about how she wasn't being rational. But again he remained silent.

"I'll run the charitable branch of your business. We'll help all kinds of people and make a difference in our community. But I will not now nor ever sit at the head of your board."

"You're saying . . . you want Preston to have the job?"

Molly knew what her dad was thinking. If she and Preston married, what difference did it make who was running the company? The business would still be in family hands. She made a hurried decision not to drop that bombshell at the same time. "Okay, yes. That's what I'm saying. I want Preston to run it."

He made a face. "And you'll run the charitable foundation?" He looked baffled, as if she might be certifiably insane to walk away from such an opportunity. "I don't have a charitable foundation."

She smiled at him again. "Exactly." Before her father could say another word, she turned around and grabbed two of her bags. "I'll meet you in the house."

That was that. He tried again later that day and the next and three times a week from then out. Molly held her ground.

Her conversation with Preston Millington was equally brief.

They grabbed coffee on the waterfront the next day, and from the moment he picked her up, she could do nothing but compare him to Ryan. He wasn't funny, and he didn't make her heart beat faster when they were together. He smelled nice, but the whole drive, he asked only a couple of questions about her. Otherwise, he was content to talk about his education, the near completion of his MBA, and his dreams for her father's corporation. He was fit and incredibly handsome, much more mature than his twenty-four years. He wore business pants and a starched white button-down, probably what her father had worn at his age. Most of that day she felt like she was talking to a one-dimensional model, fresh off the pages of *GQ* magazine.

Very quickly, she laid out the situation. "I know we had plans at one point." She took his hands in hers. "That was a long time ago. I've changed, Preston. I don't see you that way."

Preston opened his mouth as if he might refute her, but he hesitated for a long time. "Well." He sounded dazed. "I wasn't expecting that."

"You'll be okay, right?" Molly gave him a weak smile. "I mean, we've barely talked for two years. I sort of thought you'd probably moved on."

"No." It was the most thoughtful Preston had looked the whole time Molly had known him. "A guy could never just . . . move on from you, Molly."

"Thanks." She wanted to tell him he was wrong. Because Ryan was already moving on from her. He would marry his Southern belle and Molly would find her place in his past, a distant memory. This wasn't the time. "We'll be friends?"

Again he waited, but a broken smile tugged at his lips, and he shrugged. "I guess so." He exhaled in a rush. "The truth is, I'm too busy to date."

"Exactly." Molly flipped her blond hair over her shoulder. "That's what I mean. It just isn't right. You know, between us."

She convinced him with little effort, and six months later, Preston and her father helped unveil the Allen Foundation, a charity that initially brought music to orphaned children and eventually expanded to include the shelter for abandoned animals. From the first day of its existence, Molly threw herself into the foundation. The work had a healing effect on her soul. Somehow, when she was teaching a forgotten third-grader how to play the violin, she could keep from spending every waking hour wondering about her dream of the philharmonic and her thoughts about Ryan, the way she still longed for him. The way she hated him for rejecting her.

Every now and then she went to the Christian church down the street. She hoped the key to restoration lay somewhere between the altar and the doors. The pastor talked about hope and redemption and

God, the giver of second chances. Though she liked the peace she felt there, in the end she walked out of the service missing Ryan.

She believed the message. Only God could have given her a second chance with Ryan Kelly.

Three years later, with her father still harping on her to take the reins of the business, a heart attack caught up with him at a gaming table in Las Vegas. A year after they buried him, her mother died after a quick fight with cancer, and Molly couldn't get out of San Francisco fast enough.

Preston took over her father's business, and Molly moved the Allen Foundation to Portland. She began playing violin for a local theater company, and she forced her heart to move on from Nashville and Belmont and every memory of Ryan. It didn't work, of course. Not after she got settled in the Northwest and not after she found new friends and new ways to spend her free time. The memories never died. But once every twelve months, on Black Friday, she gave herself permission to go back, to relive that happiest time when all the world stood still, and to find herself again in that late-spring starry night with Ryan

Black Friday and once in a while on a rainy jog

through Portland the day after. When she couldn't quite return from the trip back to what once seemed so real. When she couldn't convince herself he wasn't waiting for her at The Bridge. When she missed him so much she could hardly breathe.

The way she felt now.

CHAPTER SIX

The hissing was getting louder.

Charlie felt like he had invisible demons on his shoulders, vicious, threatening, murderous demons, and in the last few days, their voices had gotten so loud he could barely concentrate, barely hold a conversation. He parked his '98 Chevy on the curb outside The Bridge, gathered the mail from the front seat, and went inside. Donna was out getting milk and eggs when the carrier came, so he decided to bring it here to open. As if maybe that might help sway the contents to be a little more favorable. The snow from Thanksgiving weekend had melted, but last night another storm had dumped four inches across middle Tennessee. The ground was slippery as he made his way inside.

What's the point, Charlie Barton? He could almost

sense the evil laughter in the empty storefront, the sense of despair so great it nearly consumed him. *You already know what the mail's going to say. More bad news. Just toss it in the trash and drive off a cliff. You're worthless, a failure, just like your dad predicted.*

"No." His response was audible, and it startled him. *That's not true. I won't believe that.* He gave a quick shake of his head, as if by doing so he could rid himself of the voices. Why was it so cold? He rubbed his hands together. Franklin hadn't been this cold as far back as he could remember. More snow was expected in the next few hours.

The Bridge was freezing inside, the utilities long since turned off due to nonpayment. Not that it mattered. It was Tuesday, December 11, and he was no closer to buying books for his store. No closer to finding an answer to the debt weighing him down and pressing in around him.

Which was why he'd come here this afternoon with the mail. He had submitted a loan application to the banker who once spent his free time here at The Bridge with his wife. If anyone could approve a loan, it was this man. "I have a good feeling about this, God . . . I know how You are. How You like to come through at the last minute." He laughed, the sound lost on his chattering teeth. "That's gonna happen here. I can feel it."

Charlie, you're crazy. No one would loan you money. You're not worth anything. You're a bookseller, Charlie. Banks loan money to people with a way to pay it back. Come on.

"Stop!" This time he raised his voice. "Jesus . . . give me peace. Stop the voices. Please!"

And like that, they were quiet.

His hands trembled more than before. He laid the envelopes out on his front counter. Two pieces, all that he'd brought for this moment. The first from his banker friend. The second from the company that leased him the building. Suddenly, the stone counter-top caught his attention.

As if he might find a way back to the days before the store died, Charlie spread his hands lightly over the counter. How many conversations had he shared over this piece of stone? And how many books had passed over the counter on their way to changing a life? Even saving a life? Books could do that. It was the reason Charlie believed in the bookstore.

It had saved his, after all. No other way he would

have survived the loss of their little girl, the loss of the dream of a family. His hope was found in books, and in novels of redemption and hope, purpose and true love. Through them God had given him a purpose. The purpose of putting books in the hands of other people like him.

Hurting people.

He straightened and took a deep breath. Waiting wouldn't change the contents inside the envelopes. Since only the banker's letter could contain the answer he needed, he started with the letter from the leasing company. A week ago he'd called the manager and asked for time. "The flood did me in," he told the man. "Please give me another two months to start making money. Then I'll find a way to pay you back."

The man reluctantly agreed to take the case to his supervisor. Whatever their answer, it was contained in the piece of mail in front of him. He loosened the flap with his thumb and willed his hands to be still. If only it were warmer in here. He eased the letter from the envelope and opened it. His fingers shook so much, the sound of rattling paper filled the empty space.

Dear Mr. Barton,

As per your request to extend grace in the payment of your lease, we have reached a decision. Ultimately, we would have agreed to your request. However, we have been contacted by the building's owner, and he is no longer in a position to wait on your lease payments. He has decided to sell the building, and he would like to offer it to you first.

Charlie's breath came in short bursts, and as his eyes fell on the asking price for the small house, he felt his knees start to buckle. He couldn't pay the gas bill, let alone buy the building. He skipped ahead to the next section, where the manager regretfully informed him that he had until January 1 to either leave the premises and turn in the key or make an offer on the property.

Less than three weeks.

Even with the loan, he wouldn't be able to make things right now. Although maybe he could use the loan to catch up on his back payments and convince the owner not to sell. Not yet, anyway. He felt a gasping bit of hope, and without ceremony, he grabbed the second envelope and tore it open. This one was longer and less formal.

Dear Charlie,

I love your heart for the people of Franklin, and I love your desire to keep The Bridge open. I can remember a hundred times when my wife and I hung out at your store and shared books that stirred our souls.

As a couple, there was a time when we grew busy. Life and kids and carpools and grocery shopping. We almost forgot how to love. But every time we came to The Bridge, we remembered. You and your books reminded us what was important, Charlie. I'll never forget that.

If anyone would want to loan you this money, it's me. In fact, if I had it myself, I'd be down there handing it to you. I feel that strongly. But banks don't make decisions based on emotions. I personally took your packet to our loan department, but no matter how many programs we looked at, they couldn't make the numbers work. I'm sorry, Charlie. We have to decline your application.

Please know that if anything comes up in the
future or if your situation changes, we would . . .

Charlie stopped reading and the piece of paper fell to the floor. He grabbed the edge of the counter and leaned into it to keep from falling. His chest hurt, but he wasn't having a heart attack. This was a different sort of pain. The sort of pain that came with defeat. It was a feeling as horrific as it was unrecognizable.

He would lose the store for sure, and without the loan, most likely they would lose the house, too. And then what?

Charlie worked his way to the window and clung to the frame. He rested his forehead on the cool glass and tried to grasp the severity of the blows. As he did, he remembered Donna, out buying groceries. But now she was the only one he wanted to talk to, the only voice he wanted to hear.

He pulled his cell phone from his pocket and dialed her number. They'd already lost their old cell phones. This was a pay-as-you-go phone, one they shared, and it dropped calls constantly. Still, Charlie had to try. He waited while the home phone rang, and just when he was about to give up, she answered.

"Charlie? Where are you?" Her voice held a cry of fear. "I come home from the store and you're gone."

"I came to The Bridge." He squeezed his eyes shut and drew a slow breath. "The mail came. I thought . . . I figured I'd look through it down here."

Her hesitation seemed loud and irritated even before she made a sound. "You left most of it here, by the looks of it. I'm holding seven unopened bills. Your life insurance will be the next thing to go. We can't pay it this month, Charlie."

"I know." He hated this, hated having to voice the truth to her. She had believed in him since the day they met. "Donna, we didn't get the loan. The bank . . . they had no choice, I guess. They turned us down."

"Charlie . . . no." She sounded weak and broken. As defeated as he did.

"There's more." His head was starting to hurt. He kept his eyes closed, trying to imagine the disappointment on her face. "The owner of the building is giving us until the end of the year. Then we have to be out or buy it."

"What?" Her voice was shaky, as if already tears were overtaking her. "Can they do that?"

"Yes." He tried to draw a full breath, but this time

he couldn't. The hurt in his heart was too great. He clenched his teeth, forcing the words. "I need to think. There has to be a way, Donna. Help me think of something. Maybe a banker out of town . . . or out of state. Something online where—"

"Charlie! Stop!" Though she was crying, she was angry, too. The way he had heard her get angry only a handful of times in their decades together. "Please." She lowered her voice, but the frustration remained. "It's time to walk away."

"Donna, people need bookstores. God wouldn't want me to give up on everything—"

"Look. He didn't come through this time. That means we have to figure it out on our own." She seemed more in control, less teary. "Just say your good-byes and come home. Let's figure out a way to put our lives back together."

His mind raced, searching for something to say, something to do. The answers were as nonexistent as the books in his store. What *used* to be his store. "Okay." The word pierced his heart, and when he opened his eyes, he wasn't sure he could do it, wasn't sure he could walk away from The Bridge without ever looking back. But his wife needed him. And since he could no longer make a living at his bookstore, he could at least do this.

He could come home.

The voices started in again as soon as he hung up. *Charlie, it's official. You're a failure. It was worthless. Everything you've ever done, all the people you talked to, those thousands of days you worked. The countless books you sold. Worthless. You can't even pay your life insurance.*

"No." He shook his head again, desperate for clarity.

Even Donna doesn't believe in you anymore.

"She does." He slammed his fist against the wall, and a rough sliver of wood from the window frame lodged itself in the side of his hand. "God, where are you?"

Really, Charlie? After all you've been through, you still call out to God?

"Yes." His answer sounded weak. What had Donna said? God hadn't come through for them this time, was that it? So what, then, walk away? Give up on the faith they'd clung to from the beginning? He was already halfway insane, here in this frigid empty store, talking to the voices in his head.

He remembered Donna's disappointment, how she'd made a point of telling him about the seven bills and how the life insurance would be the next to go. The bill was due before the end of the—

Suddenly, everything stopped. His breathing and his heartbeat and his reasons for despair. Before he drew his next breath, only one thought consumed him.

The life insurance.

His policy would pay off every bill they had and leave Donna enough to be comfortable the rest of her days. He looked out the window again. The snow was falling hard, the ground covered. A car accident on a day like this would be believable, right?

Of course it would be believable. Get in the car and do it, get it done. You're worth more dead than alive, Charlie. Good that you finally see that.

The voice literally hissed at him, pushing him to grab his keys. God would understand, right? He hadn't provided any way out, any answers they could stand on. He could end it tonight and never have to face Donna again, never have to see his own failure reflected in her eyes.

So get it done. What are you waiting for?

He wanted to shout at the voices, demand that they be silent. But he felt funny using Christ's name to shut them up when he was on his way to kill himself. The voices couldn't hurt him. Life . . . losing The Bridge . . . having their home foreclosed on. These were the things that could hurt him. He slid the phone back in his pocket and grabbed his keys. He knew the back roads, knew the winding routes that would cause anyone to lose control. If he did it just right, he would slip off the road and into a tree, and that would be that.

His final act of love for his precious Donna.

One last time he looked around the empty bookstore. Even now it was hard to look at it without seeing it the way it once was. Floor-to-ceiling shelves full of novels and mysteries and biographies. Customers thumbing through classics and current bestsellers, looking for the sense of adventure that had made him fall in love with books all those years ago.

He blinked back tears, breathing it in. Too many memories to take with him. Slowly, he backed out the door. At the last possible minute, he turned toward his van and shut the door behind him. Not until he was out of Franklin and headed for Leiper's Fork did he realize he'd forgotten the scrapbook. That was okay. It would be Donna's best reminder of all that had mattered to him. The scrapbook and his Bible.

Charlie felt the back tires of his van slip a little as he took the first corner. He couldn't stage just any accident. It had to be swift and deadly. Straight off a cliff and into a tree.

Make it happen, Charlie. Don't mess this up. You're worthless, a failure. Get this right, at least.

"Jesus, quiet them. Please."

As before, the voices fell silent. Chills ran down Charlie's arms, and he realized the reason more clearly than before. The name of Jesus. Evil had to flee at the sound of that name. The Bible said so. Promised it. He blinked hard and focused on the road ahead of him. There had to be a spot somewhere here, he could picture it. And in a few seconds, he knew just the spot. The sharp turn up ahead that he'd driven past many times before. The one that always made him think, *If a person weren't careful, he wouldn't make it past the curve to the other side.*

The snow fell harder, and all around the images blurred to white. White sky and trees and pavement. Even the air was solid white. The only thing he could see clearly in all the white was yesterday. He and Donna with their broken hearts, moving to Franklin and leasing the storefront. They had always liked that their business would operate from an old house.

"Our home away from home," Charlie had told her when they shared coffee and doughnuts in the empty building that first week. "And the customers will be our family."

Tears gathered in Charlie's eyes. Hope and promise, adventure and purpose. The Bridge had given them all of that, and through every stage, Donna had believed in him. She swept the place and helped patch the mortar between the bricks. She was at his side when they picked out vintage oak shelving and as he ordered new and used books. Together they had decided where fiction and history and travel books would go. Over the first few months, they had shopped antique hideaways for the living room furniture where Molly and Ryan hung out upstairs, and for the Victorian chairs that had stood for decades near the rustic brick fireplace and for the high-back tufted sofa by the front window.

When the books arrived, Donna had helped him unpack every box. With great awareness of each title's potential, they savored the process. They checked the books against their master list and found the perfect spot in the store for each. Once in a while they would take a break, sit near the fireplace, and read a few pages aloud to each other.

He would remember one particular day forever. Charlie had purchased a few early edition copies of *Treasure Island*, the book he loved most as a boy. As he lifted it from the box, he ran his fingers over the cover and stared at it. "How many kids like me have read this book and dreamed they were Jim Hawkins?" He looked at Donna, and what he saw, he had never forgotten.

Donna had tears in her eyes. Happy tears. "Have I told you lately how proud I am of you?" She took the book from him and set it carefully on the shelf. Then she put her arms around his neck and looked deep into his eyes. "This is your dream come true, Charlie. But it's more than that. Books are a love affair for you." She smiled. "Nothing could be more beautiful."

He blinked, and the image of his youthful Donna— gazing admiringly into his eyes—disappeared. He reached out after her, but his fingers connected with the cold windshield instead. What was happening? He blinked a few more times and remembered. He was driving through the snow on the winding roads toward Leiper's Fork. Driving so he could plunge off the road into a tree and—

A quick look at his speedometer grabbed his attention and brought him back to the moment. Sixty miles an hour? Into a steep downhill? He must be crazy driving this fast. Suddenly, he could see the road ahead of him more clearly. This part of the drive was lined with so many trees that the sun never hit it. He was no longer riding on snowy asphalt but on ice.

Black ice.

"No!" He shouted the word, gripping the steering wheel with both hands. He applied the brakes gently, tapping them, struggling to maintain control. But the van only flew faster down the hill.

What had he done? Donna would go to her grave brokenhearted if he ended things this way. *Please, God, I don't want to die. I love her too much.* His tears came harder, and he wiped at them with his shoulder. *God, I see the truth now. Donna might be disappointed, but we'll get through this. Don't let me die, please!* His prayer came in silent furious bursts and already he could feel the wheels beneath him sliding. "Help me, God!" Ahead of him was a tree—the tree he had pictured driving into, the trunk wider than any along this stretch of roadway. Only now he wanted to avoid it with every bit of strength he had left.

"No!" His vehicle flew down the hill out of control, heading toward a hairpin turn and the enormous tree. He slammed on his brakes because he had no other choice. No options left. The van responded by fishtailing one way and then the other until the ice whipped it around in a full spin. "God, please!"

Even as he screamed, he felt the wheels leave the hard surface and take flight. The sounds of breaking glass and crunching metal were the last he heard. Was this God's answer? Charlie would die this way, and Donna would finish her life alone? In a rush of thoughts and regrets, this one surfaced—at least he hadn't done it on purpose. The noises grew louder, and Charlie felt himself thrust against the door and the dashboard. His last thought was the saddest of all.

He hadn't told Donna he loved her.

"God!" Charlie held tight to the wheel, but the van was spinning so fast that he couldn't see anything, couldn't tell what was coming. "I'm sorry! Help me! Please . . ."

Then there was nothing but darkness.

CHAPTER SEVEN

The article in the *Tennessean* was small and otherwise insignificant. A one-column headline in reduced italic font:

Owner of The Bridge in Critical Condition
After Accident

Ryan was flipping through the newspaper when he saw it, and immediately, he felt the blood drain from his face. "No . . . not Charlie Barton." He whispered the words out loud as he raced through the ten-line article.

> Longtime owner of The Bridge bookstore,
> Charlie Barton, 59, is in critical condition
> after his van slid off an icy road in Leiper's
> Fork outside Franklin, TN, Tuesday after-

noon. Barton's vehicle struck a tree and the Jaws of Life were used to remove him from the wreckage. Barton was rushed to Vanderbilt Hospital with life-threatening injuries.

Barton and his wife, Donna, moved to Franklin in 1982 and opened The Bridge, a bookstore that has become iconic in the downtown area. The flood of 2010 gutted Barton's store, destroying its contents and sending him into apparent financial struggles. Records show that The Bridge has not reopened and that Barton's business taxes for the current year remain unpaid.

Ryan felt dizzy with the news. How had he missed this, the fact that The Bridge hadn't reopened after the flood? Other businesses had struggled to find their way back, but The Bridge? While Ryan was busy on the road, he assumed life in Franklin had figured out a way to recover. That Charlie Barton was selling books and making conversation and giving people the one thing they could find less often these days.

A bookstore to call their own.

Ryan read the article again and his heart pounded

inside his chest. Poor Charlie. The man existed to run The Bridge. He must have been desperate every day since the flood to reopen. Along the way, of course, he'd suffered financial trouble. Ryan doubted the man owned the building, so lease payments had probably piled up. An insurance policy on the store's contents wouldn't have been much help. Charlie had invested in the store's stock for decades. How could anyone put a price tag on that?

Suddenly Ryan knew what he had to do.

Charlie had spent his life helping the people of Franklin. Now it was their turn to do something for him, rally around him and let him know the difference he'd made. He pushed back from the table, grabbed his cell phone, and called Vanderbilt Hospital. "Charlie Barton's room, please."

There was a pause as the receptionist looked him up. "He's in ICU. I'll ring his nurse."

"Thank you." Ryan walked to his kitchen counter, and tapped his fingers on the granite. He needed to know the situation, how serious it was. And whether Charlie would survive or not.

A nurse came on the line. "Sixth floor, neurosurgery ICU. How can I help you?"

Ryan closed his eyes, trying to find the words. If Charlie was in the neurosurgery section, that meant he'd suffered a brain injury. Why hadn't he stopped in to see the old man since he'd been home? Ryan clenched his fist and blinked his eyes open. "I'm a friend of Charlie Barton's." He worked to keep the emotion from his voice. "Can you tell me how he is? If there's an update on his condition?"

"No, sir. I'm sorry. That information is for immediate family only."

Ryan wanted to tell her that he was one of Charlie's favorite customers, and that made him immediate family. Instead he cleared his throat. "Okay, then is Donna there? His wife?"

"She is." The woman's voice was kind, but clearly, she wasn't about to provide him any information. "Who can I tell her is calling?"

"Ryan Kelly."

She put him on hold, and after thirty seconds Ryan was thinking about hanging up and driving to the hospital, finding his way to Donna on his own. But just then her voice came on the line. "Ryan?"

"Yes." His words came in a rush. "I read about the accident. Donna, I'm so sorry." He didn't want to ask, but he needed to know before another minute went by. "How is he?"

"Not good." Tears clouded her voice. "He's unconscious. Head injuries and . . . internal bleeding."

Ryan felt the air leave his lungs. "Oh, Donna. I'm sorry." He ran his hand along the back of his neck and tried to find his next breath. "Can I come see him?"

"Yes." She sounded small and frail. "Come quickly, Ryan. Please."

"I will." He found his keys, threw on a baseball cap and a leather jacket, and hurried for the door. "I'm on my way."

The hospital was only ten minutes from his house, and Ryan was thankful the roads were clear. Along the way, it occurred to him that Donna was probably alone. If he remembered right, the Bartons had no family in Franklin other than the customers. Maybe no family anywhere. What about his injuries? What if he never woke up or the brain trauma was so severe he was never the same again? How would Donna get by without him?

As he parked and jogged toward the hospital's front entrance, he thought about calling Molly. She would want to know what happened, about the flood and Charlie's struggles and the accident. Just as quickly, he let the thought pass. He'd thought about contacting her before, but a Facebook search for Molly Allen or Molly Millington hadn't turned up anything. She must live in San Francisco with her husband, but someone in Molly's position wouldn't be found easily. Not in the past seven years and not now.

He stepped off the elevator at the sixth floor and checked in at the nursing station. "You can go in." The nurse was in her thirties, kind with serious eyes. "He's in room twelve. His wife is expecting you."

"Thank you." Ryan slowed his pace, trying to prepare for what he was about to see. When he reached Charlie's room, he removed his baseball cap and gave a light knock on the door. "Donna?"

"Come in." She sounded broken.

The entrance was blocked by a curtain. Ryan moved it aside and stepped tentatively into the room. Donna was on her feet and met him near the doorway. "Ryan." She was small and frail-looking, thinner than he remembered, and her eyes were swollen from crying.

He took her in his arms, and they hugged for a long time. "I'm sorry." Only then did he look at the figure in the hospital bed. Never would he have recognized the man as Charlie Barton. Charlie, whose smile never faded, the man who was larger than life. The one whose very presence made The Bridge what it was. His head was heavily bandaged, his face swollen beyond recognition. Half a dozen wires came from his arms and chest, and a tube had been inserted at the center of his throat. He was worse off than Ryan had imagined. *Dear God . . . help him.*

Ryan stroked Donna's back. "I came as fast as I could." He stepped back and helped her to the chair near Charlie's bed. He took the one beside her. "How is he? Really?"

Donna hung her head and for a long time said nothing. When she finally looked up, her eyes were flat. As if she'd cried all the tears she had left to cry. "They say it's a miracle he lived through the night." She looked at him, and three decades of love shone in her eyes. Then the shadows returned to her face.

"They don't know how serious his brain injury is. Even if he lives, he might never wake up."

Ryan took a sharp breath and stared at the ceiling. He wanted to run from the room and find fresh air, a place where this new reality didn't exist and he could pretend he'd never opened the newspaper this morning. But Donna needed him. He put his hand on her shoulder. "I didn't know about the flood . . . your struggles with The Bridge." He shook his head, frustrated with himself once more for not checking in on Charlie sooner.

"It's been a while." There was no accusation in her statement. She found the slightest smile. "Charlie talks about you still. He's proud of you, Ryan. You play guitar for a country band, is that right?"

"I did. The band broke up." Ryan didn't want this to be about him. He looked at Charlie's still figure beside them and then back at Donna. "The accident . . . what happened?" He hesitated. "Can you talk about it?"

Donna took a shaky breath and nodded. She folded her hands on her lap and, with her eyes on Charlie, she recalled the flood and the way it destroyed the contents of The Bridge. "The books, the furniture, the shelving. All of it." She lifted her chin, probably finding the strength not to break down. "Charlie was devastated, of course. But he always knew he'd reopen."

"Definitely. Franklin needs Charlie and the store."

"That's what we thought." Donna's eyes grew deeper, her gaze trained on her husband. "The insurance money wasn't enough." She turned to Ryan. "Without money, Charlie couldn't buy books. And without books, there was no store to open." She shrugged her slight shoulders. "No store meant no income." Her smile was beyond sad. "Charlie never had a backup plan."

Ryan hung his head and sighed. When he looked up, Donna's attention was back on Charlie. "Did things get worse lately?"

"Much." She steadied herself. "The house payment is behind, and the bank is talking foreclosure. Charlie used our savings to pay the lease on The Bridge, but that ran out over the summer. We applied for several loans, but with no working store and no income, we didn't qualify."

"And yesterday?"

"Yesterday was the worst." Though her voice didn't crack, tears filled her eyes and fell onto her cheeks. She turned to Ryan. "He had finally agreed it was time to walk away. Time to admit that there would be no more bookstore, no chance at reopening. It was over." She wiped her tears with her fingertips and leaned closer to the hospital bed, giving a quick check of the wires and tubes and monitors. "He left the bookstore for home, but he must've decided to take a drive. The accident happened five miles out of the way on a winding back road." She put her hand over Charlie's. "He must've been so upset."

Again Ryan felt like he'd been kicked. Charlie was the town's eternal optimist, always sure he could help a neighboring store owner or a customer in need. "He didn't hit another car?"

"No. He hit black ice and lost control." She ran her fingers lightly over Charlie's hand. "That's all we know."

For a while they sat in silence. Ryan stood and walked around the bed to the other side. "Can he hear us?"

"Probably not. His brain isn't showing a lot of activity yet."

Ryan picked up on the hope in Donna's choice of words. Proof that a lifetime with Charlie Barton had rubbed off on her. "Charlie." Ryan kept his voice low, bringing his head close to the older man's. "It's Ryan Kelly." He swallowed, fighting his own tears. "Hey, man, we're praying for you. It's almost Christmas, Charlie. You need to get better so we can get that store of yours up and running."

On the other side of the bed, Donna covered her face with one hand and turned away. Ryan heard her tears, anyway.

"Listen, Charlie, we're going to pull together here, okay? You just get better. God's not finished with you yet." He paused, looking for any reaction, any sign, that somewhere inside his battered head, Charlie could understand.

There was none.

Ryan backed up slowly from the bed and returned to Donna's side. Once more he hugged her and then asked her to sit back down. "I have an idea."

Donna dabbed at her tears again. "Sorry . . . I thought I was done crying."

"It's okay." He put his hand on her shoulder. "Does Charlie still have the scrapbook? He used to keep it in the top drawer near the register."

"He does." She sniffed. "Neither of us could believe it survived."

A plan began to take shape, and as it did, Ryan's heart was filled with hope. This was something he could do, something to help repay Charlie for the decades of kindness he'd given to the city of Franklin. "Is the building locked?"

She nodded. "The key's in the potted plant beside the front door. Charlie left it there so the cleanup crew could come and go after the flood. There's nothing inside for anyone to take."

"If it's okay, I'd like to go through the scrapbook and contact Charlie's customers. Let them know what happened." He didn't want to go into detail. No telling whether people would respond, and the last thing he wanted was to get Donna's hopes up.

She agreed to his plan, and before he left, he took Donna's hands in his and prayed for Charlie. For the miracle of healing and for Charlie to know the difference he'd made through his bookstore.

Half an hour later, Ryan was standing in front of The Bridge.

Traffic passed behind him and the occasional bundled-up pedestrian. Ryan barely noticed them. He stared at the sign over the door, the old lettering that might as well have been something from a Charles

Dickens novel. THE BRIDGE—NEW AND USED BOOKS. Ryan stared at it, and for a moment it wasn't the middle of December, and the store on the other side of the door wasn't gutted. It was seven years ago and springtime and Molly was at his side.

He blinked away the images, found the key, and walked in. The sight made him catch his breath. The place was unrecognizable. Even the single piece of furniture—an old leather sofa—wasn't the one that had been here. He closed the door and leaned hard against it. No wonder Charlie had been broken. No wonder he couldn't focus when he left here yesterday.

A quick search, and he found the scrapbook, the treasured collection of notes and thank-you letters and signatures from hundreds of special customers over the years. The cover of the oversize book was water-damaged, but the inside looked intact. Ryan was about to leave when he caught a glimpse of the staircase. The one that led to what had been the upstairs living room, the place where he and Molly had spent two years of afternoons.

He set the book down on the counter and walked gingerly across the wood floor. It creaked more loudly than before, and some areas didn't feel quite solid.

How hard it must've been for Charlie, knowing he couldn't repair the planks, couldn't fix the walls and fill the building with the books he loved. Ryan walked up the stairs, and each one seemed to take him further back into the past. The upstairs looked as bad as the main floor, the furniture gone, the place painfully empty. Just like Donna had said.

Ryan couldn't stay, couldn't stand to breathe in the dank musty air where once life had shone so brightly. He took a final look and returned to the counter for the scrapbook. Then he drove home and sat at his desktop computer. It was time to get busy.

Time to tell Charlie Barton's family what had happened.

━━━

The opening page of Charlie's scrapbook doubled Ryan's determination. The book was a gift from Edna Carlton, a woman Ryan didn't know. But her words gave him a single-minded purpose. She wrote that The Bridge had given her a second chance at life.

It was exactly what Charlie needed. A second chance.

Ryan made a few phone calls and easily convinced the owner of Sally's Mercantile to set up a donation center for anyone wanting to help Charlie. He worked through the scrapbook like a detective, and by three o'clock that afternoon he had written private Facebook messages to thirty-seven former customers of The Bridge. His message was the same to all:

You don't know me, but we have something in common. At one point we found solace at Charlie Barton's bookstore in downtown Franklin. The Bridge made a difference for me, and I know it made a difference for you because I found your name in Charlie's scrapbook of customers.

People he considered family.

Now Charlie is in trouble. He was in a serious car accident yesterday afternoon and today he's fighting for his life at Vanderbilt Hospital in Nashville. That's not all. The Bridge suffered devastating damage in the flood that hit eighteen months ago. Charlie tried to reopen, but he didn't have the funds or the books and the place remains closed. The accident happened after Charlie had given up all hope of ever opening his doors again.

I'm not sure how you can help. But I'm asking you to join me in praying for a miracle for Charlie Barton. The miracle of a second chance. Beyond that, if you're in the area, there's a donation drop-off set up at Sally's Mercantile. We're looking for books, new, old, used, anything you can give. I'd like Charlie to wake up to more books than he knows what to do with.

Charlie loved all of us. Now it's our turn to love him.

Sincerely, Ryan Kelly

Ryan felt his hope rising. Certainly, this many people could make a difference. But by late that evening he was deeply discouraged. Though he checked every hour, none of the former customers had responded. Then Donna called with an update. Charlie was clinging to life, but he'd made no improvements. *Please, God . . . don't let it end this way for Charlie.* Ryan stayed by his laptop through the night, but by the time he turned in, he had heard from only two customers, both of whom promised to pray. But since they now lived out of the area, they couldn't do much more.

What good could possibly come from such a weak response? The prayers were great, but where would the books come from? Ryan felt drained physically and emotionally. He would try again tomorrow, contact the *Tennessean* about the city getting behind a book drive for The Bridge, and maybe try to find the rest of the customers. He was surprised how many weren't on Facebook, but maybe if he Googled their names, he'd get further. Even then he doubted he'd find the one person he was desperate to find. The person who would care about Charlie Barton's tragedy as much as he did. The girl he had thought about every hour of that sad day.

Molly Allen.

CHAPTER EIGHT

The week before Christmas was insanely busy at the animal rescue shelter. Parents needed gifts for their kids, and by that Friday, four days before Christmas, lots of people were practically desperate. A rescued pet was often the perfect solution. That and the fact that hearts were softer this time of year—more willing to help, more open to visiting the shelter and leaving with a cat or dog.

Molly hadn't seen so many animals leave with homes since she'd opened the foundation. Even better, she had authorized fourteen music scholarships for kids from foster homes. A music scholarship came only after a child had been a part of the Allen Foundation's music development program through high school. The years of work with her foundation were paying off. Lives were being changed.

The work had been arduous, since Molly liked to be in on researching each scholarship application and the extent of the need. Still, as she walked into her apartment late that afternoon, as she shook off her umbrella and flipped on the lights, she felt more satisfied than she had all month. She brewed a pot of coffee and opened a can of food for her cat.

"It's going to be a good Christmas, Sam." She liked to tell the cat things like that. Saying them out loud made them easier to believe.

Sam meowed in her direction and turned his attention to his food bowl.

Molly pulled out her phone and checked her schedule. She had a show tonight with the children's theater, a performance of *The Nutcracker*. Call time was in two hours. She could hardly wait to be surrounded by the music, lost in the story. The play's director had pulled her aside after the first rehearsal. "You have the talent to play first violin." She'd raised her brow. "But you don't have enough time. Or do you?"

"I don't." Molly had appreciated the compliment. She might not have made it to the New York Philharmonic, and she might never play Carnegie Hall, but she had never let her dream die. Tonight she would play second violin.

She smiled. Ryan would have been happy about that, at least.

Her coffee was ready. Molly poured herself a steaming mug, added an inch of organic half and half, and sat down at the kitchen counter. She picked up her phone and thumbed her way to the Twitter app. Time didn't allow her to check in often, but it was one way to stay in touch with people in the music business, as well as contacts and friends she'd made in Portland. Facebook was too time-consuming, but Twitter was doable.

She scrolled down the timeline, smiling at the occasional reference to shopping frenzies at the mall and failed attempts at wrapping gifts. Then something caught her eye. Maybe out of nostalgia for the past, Molly followed @VisitFranklin—a Twitter account that kept her posted on the happenings of the town she once loved. Somewhere in her heart, she probably hoped to see occasional updates on The Bridge or Ryan Kelly, but that never happened and she generally breezed over the town's posts.

This one made her set her coffee down, made her

breathing quicken. The tweet didn't contain much information, but it was enough.

Charlie Barton, owner of The Bridge, still in ICU after car accident. Find out how you can help. At the end of the tweet was a link, and Molly clicked it, her heart skittering into a strange rhythm. Charlie Barton? In ICU? A website opened with a photo of Charlie and another of The Bridge. The headline read FRANKLIN RALLIES IN SUPPORT OF LOCAL BOOKSTORE OWNER. Molly stared at it and then at the pictures.

It wasn't until she started reading the article that she gasped out loud. Once she got past the details of Charlie's accident and the devastating effects of the Nashville flood on his store, she reached the part about the book drive.

> The effort is spearheaded by Ryan Kelly, one of Barton's longtime customers and a resident of Nashville. Kelly is a professional guitarist who spent the last five years touring with one of the nation's top country bands.

Molly read the line two more times. She felt a smile start in her heart and work its way to her face. "You did it, Ryan . . . you chased your dream." She spoke to the article as if he could hear her. He had done what he told her he'd do, and now he was the one leading the charge for Charlie Barton. Sadness came over her again. She would do whatever she could to help Charlie. At the bottom of the article was information on how to reach Ryan, a Facebook link, and the phone number of Sally's Mercantile.

She checked the time. It was two hours later in Nashville, too late to do anything now. As she finished her coffee and dressed for the show, she couldn't stop thinking about what had happened. The flood and Charlie Barton's accident and Ryan's determination to repay the man for his contribution to the people of Franklin. He had probably married his Mississippi girl and moved her to middle Tennessee. By now he might have a family, two or three children.

As she took her seat for second violin and the opening performance of the weekend run, as she felt the music come to life beneath her fingertips, she was comforted by one thought. For all she didn't know about Ryan Kelly, she knew this much. Their time together at The Bridge had to count for something.

Because he had followed his dream.

Tchaikovsky's music spoke to Molly the way it always did. This time it swept her from the small theater into the past, to the days when she first studied the composer at Belmont University. When they reached the second act and the song for Clara and her prince charming, Molly felt like she was playing a soundtrack to every wonderful moment she'd ever shared with Ryan.

The haunting strains of the violin seemed to cry out the question wracking her heart, the one that wouldn't leave her alone. What had happened? How could he have kissed her that way, held her so closely, and looked at her with the certainty that their friendship had turned a corner? How could he have been so convincing in his feelings for her and then apologized the next day?

One song led to the next, and with every stanza, a plan began to form. She needed to get to Franklin, to the hospital room of Charlie Barton. She had two performances tomorrow, but Sunday was open. She could fly to Nashville in the morning and be at Charlie's bedside before nightfall. Her staff could carry on here, and she could fly home Christmas Eve.

There was one problem.

She had no idea what to do if she ran into Ryan. His pity, his apology, had been part of the reason why she'd left Belmont and made her father happy by returning home. She couldn't stay at school knowing Ryan didn't share her feelings. Her heart would've broken again every day. Ryan had chosen the girl back home over her. She had no way around that fact.

So what about now? How would she feel running into him, seeing his wife on his arm, and facing the awkward moments that were bound to follow? As the ballet ended, she thought of a way. It wouldn't protect her heart, but it would protect her from his sympathy. She'd do what other girls had done to look taken, what her receptionist did when she went out with friends just so guys wouldn't hit on her. It might've been an old ploy and a little outdated, but it would get her through the weekend.

She would wear her mother's wedding ring.

He would think she'd gone home and fallen hard for Preston, and he wouldn't question her, wouldn't feel sorry for her. In that way—and only in that way—could she work alongside him and his wife. She could do her part to help Charlie Barton. Maybe she could even find a way to tell him she was sorry, add her apology to his. She could let him know that she never meant for their friendship to cross lines. It was a crazy idea then, and it seemed even crazier now. In light of where life had taken them.

If she apologized like that, then maybe in time her heart would follow. She could come to believe that their spring night together had been a mistake, and she could find a way to live again. Really live. Without the video or the memories or the Black Friday ritual.

She booked the flight that night, and first thing Sunday morning, she moved her small suitcase by the front door and called for her ride. The last thing she took was the one thing she could donate to the community efforts for Charlie Barton, a book she no longer needed.

Her copy of *Jane Eyre*.

That night after she landed in Nashville and checked into her hotel, she took a walk to the church across the street. With every step, she looked for him, watched for Ryan the way she once searched for him in her dreams. Did he live here near the airport or closer to Franklin? Molly wasn't sure, but Ryan wasn't the only thing clouding her mind.

She had called the hospital and talked to Donna Barton. The news on Charlie wasn't good. He remained in a coma, on a ventilator. Every day his chances of waking up grew slimmer. Molly walked through the back doors of the church. The place was empty, and Molly found a spot in one of the back pews. Quietly, reverently, she dropped to her knees.

Her hands shook and her heart raced along in time with her desperate thoughts. She wasn't used to praying or especially good at it. For all she knew, she was going about it all wrong, so she did the only thing she knew to do. Lacing her fingers together, she closed her eyes. *God, if You're really there . . . I think I'll just talk to You like a friend. I don't know what else to do.* Her lips were dry, and she felt a shiver run down her arms. She liked that, thinking of God as a friend. A friend she very much needed right now. She twisted her mother's wedding ring, the one newly on her left hand. *I really need Your help. For Charlie Barton, so that he'll live . . . and so that I'll have the right words if I run into Ryan.*

That was it. She didn't have much else to say. This last part was the most important of all, so she whispered the words out loud. "And if You're really the God of second chances, maybe You could stay with Charlie Barton. Because no one needs a second chance right now more than he does."

When she finished her prayer, she stood and called for another ride. Tomorrow she would visit Sally's Mercantile and see how she could help with the book drive. She still had one more destination before the night was over.

Vanderbilt Hospital.

Donna had started a CaringBridge page, a way to keep people updated about Charlie's progress, his physical condition, and the ways they could help. She sat beside Charlie's bed in the dimly lit hospital room and used a loaner laptop to check the page's guest-book for the first time.

What she saw shocked her. She had no idea how Ryan had garnered so much support, but already Charlie's site had over a thousand views and nearly two hundred comments. Donna started at the begin-ning, and chills ran down her arms and neck.

*Donna, you don't know us, but we're pray-
ing for you. A few years ago my husband and I
came to The Bridge looking for information
about adoption. Charlie led us to a couple of
books, which we purchased at a discount.
Charlie insisted. One of the books told about
how to survive the process of adoption. The
other told the fictional story of one couple's
journey to add a child to their family. Those
books changed our lives. We live in Atlanta
now and last month we welcomed home twin
little girls from China. Our plan was to bring
them to The Bridge so they could meet Charlie.
Please know that everything your husband has
done with that bookstore mattered. It mattered
to the people of Franklin and it mattered to us.
When he wakes up, let him know. God bless
you.*

"Charlie, listen to—" She looked up, excited, before
she caught herself. She'd done this more than once.
Forgotten that he was in a coma, that he couldn't hear
her. As quickly as she chose not to share with him, she
changed her mind. What if he could hear her?

Wouldn't it be better for him to know the difference he'd made?

With steady hands and a strong voice, she read the woman's entry out loud. "Can you believe that, Charlie?" She slid her chair closer and took hold of his limp hand. "Two little girls have a family because of your books. That's amazing."

Her joy continued as she shared one post after another. Nothing had filled her heart so completely since Charlie's accident. There was a note from a young woman who had talked with Charlie ten years ago about her broken relationship with her mother.

"'Charlie gave me a novel about forgiveness and told me it would make me see things differently. I wanted to read it, but I was broke. I asked if I could stop by the store and read it in stages and Charlie only smiled. He told me I could have the novel for a dollar. I read the book and when I finished the last chapter I hit my knees. I asked God to forgive me and then I called my mom and asked her to do the same.'" Donna hesitated, overcome by the happiness in her heart. She cleared her voice and continued. "'My husband and I live near her now in Oklahoma. I feel like everything about my current situation can somehow be traced back to that single conversation, that kind act. I've never seen a bookseller love books more than Charlie Barton. Please let him know we are praying. Our church is collecting new and used books. After Christmas I'll drive the carload down there myself. It's the least I can do.'"

One after another, for an hour straight, Donna read the entries to Charlie. His breathing pattern didn't change. He didn't stir or show eye movement or flex the muscles in his hand. But Donna believed with all her heart that somehow he could hear her. The posts were like people lined up in the room, each of them giving Charlie a reason to believe.

A reason to wake up and find a way to keep The Bridge.

She was about to read another post when there was a sound at the door. Donna looked up as a tall young woman walked in. Her long blond hair fell in a perfect sheet against her dark coat, and Donna was struck by her beauty, despite her deeply troubled face. Her ice blue eyes and fine features looked familiar.

"Hello." Donna set the laptop on the table and stood to meet the woman, trying to place her.

"Mrs. Barton?"

The young woman's voice helped, because in a rush, Donna had the answer. "Molly Allen!" She went to the young woman and hugged her. "It's been so long."

"It has. Too long." Molly looked past Donna to the hospital bed. "I had to come."

"Thank you." For all the light that the CaringBridge entries had cast across the room, and even with the joy of seeing Molly, the truth remained. "He's very bad off."

"I'm sorry." She walked slowly to the bed and grabbed hold of the side rail. "Charlie, it's me. Molly Allen." She waited, the way all of Charlie's visitors waited. As if this might be the moment when he would open his eyes and smile and they'd all have him back. Charlie remained motionless. Molly turned to Donna. "Is he . . . any better?"

"No. He's alive, but we've had no improvement since the accident."

Molly looked like she might cry.

"Did Ryan get hold of you? Is that why you're here?" Donna and Charlie always believed that the two college students belonged together. Neither ever heard what happened, why Molly had gone back to California.

"No." She smiled, and a shyness filled her eyes. "I haven't talked to Ryan since I left. I heard about Charlie on the Internet. Through Twitter."

"Hmm. So many people talking about him. He would be amazed. How many lives he's touched."

Molly nodded, and for a few minutes she sat and talked with Donna. Told her about the foundation and how she played violin for a local orchestra.

"So you haven't seen Ryan?" Donna asked.

"No." Molly smiled again, patient with the questions. "Has he been up here?"

"Every day. Several times a day, actually." Donna settled back in her chair. "If you come back tomorrow, I'm sure you'll see him."

"I'm sure." Molly looked at her watch. "I need to get to the hotel. I'll head to downtown Franklin tomorrow. See if I can help. Then I'll be back." She stood and hugged Donna.

"Thank you . . . for coming." Donna looked at her husband. "I have to believe that somehow, deep inside Charlie's brain, he knows what is happening. How people are coming together and praying for him." She smiled. "Even flying in from across the country to be here."

"I believe that, too." Molly waved once more, and then she was gone.

Donna wanted to tell Molly that Ryan was single, that he was a wonderful young man, and that maybe it wasn't too late for the two of them. But at the last moment she noticed something she hadn't before, something that put an end to the thought before she could give it a voice.

The wedding ring on Molly's left hand.

CHAPTER NINE

Ryan knew it was her the moment he walked into the Mercantile.

Her long blond hair, same as it had been back at Belmont, the graceful way she had about her, and the sound of her voice. That most of all. He stopped in the doorway and stared, just stared at her. Like he was seeing a vision, not the real Molly Allen. How had she heard about Charlie and why had she come?

When she had left so easily that long-ago summer?

He took a few steps into the building, ignoring the bustle of last-minute shoppers crowding the aisles of the store. He thought about saying nothing, just standing there and taking in the sight of her. But he couldn't keep himself from her, couldn't let this much distance come between them for another minute. "Molly . . ."

She must not have heard him, because she kept talking, and only then did Ryan realize what she was doing. Molly was dropping off several bags of new books, helping the store owner arrange them in big boxes until they were overflowing with books. He watched her for a moment and then came closer. "Molly?"

This time there was no hesitation. She turned, and for the first time in more than two thousand sunsets, her eyes met his. He had wondered if he would know her as fully if they ever had a moment like this. Whether she would've changed somehow and the connection they once shared would only be one more part of the memory. But now he could see that wasn't the case. In her eyes he watched her shock turn to elation, then temper to something more appropriate, given their hasty good-bye and the years between them.

"Ryan." She uttered a quiet laugh, clearly more breathless than amused. "I wondered if I'd see you."

"You look . . . beautiful." He closed the distance between them, and despite the store owner and customers, he took hold of her hands, their eyes connected as if all of time had led to this moment. But as he held her fingers in his, as he savored the softness of her skin, he felt something else.

Her wedding band.

He released her hands and moved back enough to keep things appropriate. She was a married woman now, and he couldn't let the thrill of seeing her consume him. Her father had been wrong in what he'd told Ryan seven years ago. But here, the man would be right. Ryan had no right to confuse her. Not when she was married.

The floor beneath him shifted as he caught her eyes again. How could she have gone to someone else after the bond they shared? The kiss that night? He steadied himself. "How . . . how'd you hear?"

"Twitter." Her smile was sad, but there was something in her eyes he couldn't quite read. Regret, maybe, or wistfulness. The result of remembering. "I had to come."

Ryan had to keep things on a surface level. He wouldn't survive otherwise. "Looks like you bought a few books."

"I did." She walked back to the counter, and he followed. "Every book I could remember seeing on the shelves at The Bridge."

He sorted through the contents. They were brand-new, but they were classics. *Little Women* and *Tom Sawyer* and *The Call of the Wild*. What looked like the entire C. S. Lewis collection. "I'd say this is a great start."

"It's hardly the start." She pointed to the boxes on the floor behind the register. "You did a good job, Ryan. Word's getting out."

"You can say that again." Sally, the storeowner, walked up, tying her apron around her waist. "These boxes weigh a hundred pounds each. Four of them here and another five in the back. When we're through with this drive, Charlie Barton will need two storefronts."

A flicker of sadness made its way through Ryan. Charlie would need them only if he woke up. For now it was easier to believe that his only problem was re-stocking The Bridge. If not for Charlie, then for Donna. In case she might want to run the store. It was something tangible that the town could get behind, since there was nothing any of them could do to help Charlie recover.

That part was in God's hands.

Molly was grateful for the wedding ring. The moment their eyes met, everything she'd ever felt for him came bursting to the surface. Only the feel of the ring on her finger kept her from gushing about how much she'd missed him and how great it was to see him again.

He must have noticed it, because a few seconds after taking hold of her fingers, he stepped away. Which was only right, since he was married, too. At least she assumed he was. He was wearing a ring. But as she helped him load one of the nine boxes into the back of his truck, she realized it wasn't on his left hand. *Strange,* she thought. Either way, she was glad she had worn a ring. Glad he thought she was married. It was probably why things didn't seem awkward between them. He didn't have to be sorry anymore. Not if she was happy in her new life.

Even if the ring represented nothing but a lie.

On the trip out to the parking lot with the second box, she nearly fell when her foot got stuck in a pothole. She cried out but caught herself before she hit the ground. "Wow, that was close."

"Graceful as ever." He grinned at her. "Remember the time when you fell down the stairs at the music building?"

"Yes. Apparently not as well as you remember it." She adjusted the grip on her half of the box, and they continued on to his truck. "Where are we taking them?"

"To the hospital." He set his edge of the box on the open tailgate, easily hopped into the bed, and slid the box to the back with the other one.

"Really?" She brushed a bit of dirt off the lower part of her jeans. "Is there room?"

"For now. The staff said we could keep the books lined up on one side of the room until tomorrow. Christmas Eve. Then we can move them to my storage unit. I have room." His heart hurt again. "We're all praying for a miracle."

"Definitely."

"That Charlie will wake up and see the books"—he jumped back down to her level—"the day before Christmas. And he'll know how much we care. How much The Bridge mattered."

"Hmmm." She walked beside him as they headed back for the next box. "Why not take the books to the store?"

Ryan felt the weight of her question. "The Bartons have until the first of the year before they have to clear out."

"The first?" She stopped and stared at him. "What happens then?"

"You didn't hear?" He dug his hands in his back pockets. The explanation clearly pained him. She could see that. "The owner is selling the building. If he can't buy it, they want him out. There's a for-sale sign in the window."

Molly felt her shoulders slump. "Then what's the point if he won't have a store?"

"We have to start somewhere." Ryan's smile was bittersweet, the same one he'd given her when she left him way back when. "That's what Scarlett O'Hara would say, right?"

For a moment she wasn't standing here a few days before Christmas, pretending to be married. She was back in her car, driving him to The Bridge and laughing about the plot twists in *Gone with the Wind*. She smiled, and for the first time in years, she felt nineteen again. "Yes. That is what she'd say."

They finished loading the boxes and then drove them to Vanderbilt Hospital. Together they got them through the front door, and Ryan found a dolly. Four trips later, they walked up to Donna, winded from the effort.

"This is unbelievable." Donna put her hand to her mouth, her eyes wide. "I can't believe it. Every one of those books was brought in for Charlie?"

"There's more." Ryan chuckled. "Lots more."

"Amazing." Donna looked like she wasn't sure whether she should laugh or cry. Instead she hugged each of them. "Seeing you here together. Everything feels like it's going to be okay."

"It is." Ryan looked at the boxes stacked against the far wall. He moved closer to the hospital bed. "You need to wake up, Charlie. You have books to stock." Ten seconds passed, but Charlie didn't move, didn't give any sign whatsoever that he could hear. Slowly Ryan turned away and looked at Donna. "Any improvements?"

"Actually, yes." Though the corners of her lips lifted a little, her eyes remained worried. "The doctor said he's seen more brain activity. He tried to let Charlie breathe on his own, but that didn't last long. A couple minutes, maybe."

"That's more than before. Ask the doctor to try that

again." Molly looked from Donna to Charlie and back. The hospital scene was painfully familiar. "I remember when my mom was sick, especially at the end. A doctor needs to be encouraged, working with patients like Charlie. Patients need an advocate, Donna. Seriously."

Donna nodded, listening. "I don't want him to get worse."

"Then keep pushing for them to take him off the ventilator. Being on the vent, that's what makes patients sicker."

"I've heard that," Ryan agreed. "Pneumonia can set in. Molly's right. The sooner they get him breathing on his own, the better."

"Okay." Donna looked more determined. "I'll call for the doctor as soon as you leave."

"Perfect." Ryan hesitated. "Before we leave, let's pray."

Again Molly wasn't sure how to feel. But if Ryan was leading, she was content to listen. He held his hands out to her and Donna, and the three of them formed a tight circle. Ryan asked God to breathe healing into Charlie's lungs and give him the strength to fight for life. Molly caught most of the words, but she was distracted. Not by the feel of her hand in Ryan's larger one. But because while he prayed, an idea came to her.

Maybe the best idea she'd ever had.

They weren't quite in the elevator when Molly turned to him, her excitement bursting. "I know how I can help Charlie."

"How?" He looked mildly amused. As if this might be another of her wild plans, like having him over for dinner that night in Brentwood.

"Ryan!" She didn't want him mocking her. "I'm serious." Her tone sounded wounded, but she kept her expression relaxed. So he wouldn't know her real feelings. "Take me to The Bridge."

"Now?" They had planned to go back to Sally's Mercantile for the rest of the books.

"Yes, now." She smiled, and it felt wonderful. Even if everything about this day together was pretend. "Come on. It won't take long."

"Fine." He chuckled but didn't seem to mind. Besides, the drive would give them a chance to catch up. "I guess it's only fitting, huh? You and I driving from this neighborhood down Franklin, to the Bridge."

She hadn't thought about that. "Can you . . . take the detour? Through campus?"

He hesitated. "Are you sure?" His look said he wasn't, that maybe this was more than either of them could take. But then he was the one who had apologized. He'd seen her only as a friend, so what harm could there be in going back? Just this once.

"Very sure."

They reached his truck and climbed inside. The hospital was a mile from Belmont. Ryan drove south on Twenty-first, left on Wedgewood, and right on Belmont Circle, through the heart of the campus. Neither of them said anything as he drove slowly past Fidelity Hall and the music business center, past McWhorter Hall and Massey Performing Arts Center. Every building, every stretch of sidewalk the two of them had walked and talked and laughed along.

At one point he nearly stopped, clearly as caught up in the remembering as she was. "It feels like yesterday."

"I guess I never thought it would end."

"Yeah . . ." He gave her a strange look but then turned his attention back to the campus. "I thought I was the only one who felt that way."

His comment seemed deeper than the words seemed to imply. Molly couldn't begin to sort through the reason or the meaning.

Ryan circled up to Caldwell and east to Twelfth. From there it was easy to get to Franklin Road. They'd done the drive a few hundred times together. She angled herself so she could study him, the man he had become. "I hear you're famous."

"What?" He looked at her once, and then again, before turning his attention back to the road. "Who says that?"

"The article on Twitter. You play guitar for one of the nation's top country acts."

"I did play." His laugh sounded self-deprecating. "Now I'm just an unemployed famous guitar player."

Her laughter joined his. "Not for long."

"It's been a few weeks."

"Sounds like you could use the break." She smiled, proud of him, regardless of the way he'd hurt her so long ago. Never mind her heartache. He had followed his dream, and she was happy for him. "Did your wife go with you on the road?"

Again he gave her the strangest glance, then a slight shake of his head. "No wife." They reached a red light, and he turned to her. "What made you think I was married?" He sounded more baffled than amused. "Twitter say that, too?"

"No." She had to tread lightly here. She didn't want to take the conversation too far back. "I just thought . . . I mean—" She felt her face getting hot. "You were in love with her, Ryan. She waited for you for two years."

"I cared about her." His eyes held hers. "But I wasn't in love with her."

She looked away first, turned her eyes to the road ahead of them. The light turned green and he did the same. "So you never married?"

"No." He thought for a few seconds. "I barely had time to date between show runs."

"Hmmm." Her heart took the blow, and a handful of emotions filled her senses, stopping her from saying anything else. He had never married, and yet he'd never called her? Had he cared that little for her? It was one thing to think he'd apologized for kissing her because he was in love with the girl back home. This was something entirely different: the idea that he would rather be single than pursue her.

"You okay?" He moved like he might reach for her hand, then he stopped himself. "You're quiet."

"Just thinking." She didn't look at him, couldn't take the way her heart would betray her if she did. "All this time . . . I pictured you married. Maybe with two or three kids by now."

"Nope. Twenty-eight and single." He leaned back, squinting against the glare of the snow on the fields surrounding Franklin Road. "And you, Molly? I assume you're happy?"

She thought for a few seconds. If he came out and asked her, she wouldn't lie. His question assumed she was married, so she let the ruse remain. Better than having him pity her. "Yes. I'm in Portland now."

"Oregon?" He seemed as surprised as she had been a few minutes ago. "I thought you were in San Francisco."

"A lot's changed." She hoped he couldn't hear her pounding heart. "My dad died four years ago. Cardiac arrest. My mom passed away a year after that from cancer."

"Molly . . . I didn't know." His expression softened, and this time he put his hand on her shoulder. "I'm sorry."

"I wasn't close to them. You know that."

"Still . . ." He paused, as if he didn't want to rush the moment. "So what happened to your dad's company?"

"Preston runs it." She wouldn't have been surprised if her heart burst from her chest, it was beating so hard. "I run the Allen Foundation. Transferred it to the Northwest." Though she still hadn't lied, she was close.

Ryan nodded, thoughtful. "So it all worked out. Just like your father wanted."

She didn't deny the fact. If he didn't care enough to call after sending her away with his apology, then he didn't deserve the details.

Neither that nor the truth.

———

They pulled up in front of The Bridge and stepped onto the snowy curb. Someone had cleared the sidewalks, apparently, and even on this late Sunday afternoon, shoppers were making their way along the row of quaint stores and boutiques. Molly didn't want to think about the past for another minute. But here, there was no way around it.

She spotted the for-sale sign in the window, pulled out her cell phone, and snapped a picture.

"I know. I did the same thing," Ryan's voice was heavy, a reflection of his heart. "One of these days the sign will be down. I figured I'd get my picture while I could."

"Exactly." She checked the photo as she followed him to the front door. It was perfectly clear, easy to read the phone number on the sign. She waited while he found the key in a plant beside the door, and they walked inside. Tears stung her eyes as she looked around. She leaned back against the cold brick wall. "I don't know what I expected. But this is worse."

"He lost everything." Ryan walked around the front counter and opened the drawer. "His scrapbook. The one with all his favorite customers."

"His family . . . that's what he called us." She stood opposite Ryan and ran her fingers over the book.

"I used this to find some of the people through Facebook." He gave her a wry look. "Not you, obviously. I wasn't sure what name you were using."

"I'm not on Facebook." Again she tiptoed around her reality. "Too busy."

"Just Twitter, huh?" He smiled at her.

"Mm-hm. Less upkeep." She couldn't take looking

into his eyes. With a quick breath, she turned and walked across the front room to the fireplace. Her eyes followed the stairs up to the second floor. "He can't lose this place."

"Which reminds me." Ryan came to her and stopped a few feet away. "What's your idea?"

"Idea?" She felt her face go blank and she gave him a guilty smile. "I guess I forgot."

Again his expression told her he wasn't sure about the way she was acting. "You sure you're okay?"

"Yes." She laughed. "Let's get back to the Mercantile. We need to get a few more books back to the hospital so Charlie sees them when he wakes up."

She loved turning the focus back to the book drive, back to something real and tangible they could do for Charlie Barton. Molly believed he would wake up. That had to be why his brain was showing more function. The hope that lay in the next twenty-four hours made her trip to Nashville worthwhile, and it dulled the ache in her heart for the one thing she didn't want to think about. Not then and not the next morning, when a group of customers gathered at the Mercantile to pray for Charlie.

If Ryan wasn't married, why hadn't he called?

CHAPTER TEN

Donna couldn't take her eyes off the books. Nine boxes delivered by Molly and Ryan yesterday and another three this morning. She had done a rough count and the number nearly dropped her to her knees. The townspeople of Franklin had collected almost as many books as Charlie had intended to buy. Not only that, but some people had donated cash with notes like the one she'd just read: *You gave me my first book for free, something I never forgot. Back then you told me I could pay for it whenever I had the money. Well, Charlie Barton, I have the money now. Lots of it. So here's a thousand dollars. Keep your bookstore open. We need it—all of us.*

Good thing Ryan had room in his storage unit for them. He'd arranged a group of people to move them the day after Christmas.

Altogether, nearly two thousand dollars had been collected and tucked into the boxes of donations. All that, and the books were not just any titles. In many cases, they were the books they once purchased at The Bridge, or copies of their favorite fiction and true-life titles. Many of the books held messages—another of Ryan's ideas. Like the messages in Charlie's Caring-Bridge, the inscriptions in the books were enough to get Donna through the day, enough to keep her believing for a miracle.

If people loved Charlie enough to do this, then maybe God wasn't finished with him. She could only pray she was right. Especially now, late on the morning of Christmas Eve.

Donna moved closer to Charlie's bedside. "Hello, Charlie." She smiled, studying the lines on his face, willing his eyes to open. "Merry Christmas."

He didn't make a sound. But something in his expression seemed to change. She waited, watching. "You breathed on your own for half an hour this morning." With all the love she had for the man in the hospital bed, she stood and kissed his forehead, touching her lips gently to his forehead. "I love you,

Charlie. Please, honey, wake up." She kissed him once more, on the cheek this time. "I need you."

The sound of voices came from the hallway, and Donna turned around. Carolers, maybe. Charlie's nurse had told her that sometimes on Christmas Eve or Christmas Day, church groups would come through the halls singing. As the voices drew near, Donna was sure that's what this was. Carolers. The song was "O Holy Night," and the refrain filled the sixth-floor ICU.

"O holy night . . . the stars are brightly shining . . . this is the night of our dear Savior's birth."

Donna looked at her husband's still form. "Did you hear that, Charlie? This is the night. It's Christmas Eve, Charlie."

Suddenly, his right hand moved. Not much and not for long, but Donna was convinced. He had moved his hand! Could that mean he was coming out of the coma? She rang for his nurse.

"Yes?"

"He's moving. I promise, I saw his hand move!"

"Yes, Mrs. Barton. Someone will be right in."

Donna turned to watch the door, overwhelmed

and shaking from the possibility. The carolers were getting closer, singing about a thrill of hope and the weary world rejoicing. All Donna could think was there couldn't be a better song for the backdrop of what might be happening at this very moment.

The possibility that Charlie was waking up.

Instead of passing by the room, the carolers filed in. First two, and then three more, and then an entire stream of carolers. Tears filled Donna's eyes, and she sat slowly by her husband's hospital bed, unable to take it all in. They hadn't come for the hospital wing; they had come for Charlie. Donna figured it out when the last of the singers entered the room.

Molly and Ryan.

Ryan winked at her and kept up the song, filling the room with a message of a new and glorious morn. When they reached the part about falling on their knees, Donna saw Charlie move again. Both hands this time. She remembered stories in the Bible where victory came when the people sang. There had never been a song more beautiful than this.

Donna looked from face to face, and another realization hit her. This wasn't a church group coming to cheer Charlie up. These were his customers. Her hand flew to her mouth, tears streaming down her face as she recognized the people who had donated books and money. They had found a way here to sing about the greatest miracle of all.

The miracle of baby Jesus in a manger.

Again Donna saw Charlie move, this time his right foot. This night was as divine as the one Charlie's customers were singing about. Because only the touch of God could stir life back into Charlie after all these days. The song came to an end, and Ryan stepped forward. "We spent the morning praying for Charlie. That he would wake up." He put his hand on Charlie's foot. "A few of us figured he might want a Christmas song to wake up to."

Donna dabbed at her tears. "You sounded wonderful." She looked at Charlie again. "He's . . . been moving. For the last few minutes."

———

Charlie heard the noises, heard them blurring and mixing together. Darkness surrounded him, and he wondered if he were dead, if he were in some stage before he would meet the Lord. His head hurt, and he felt stuck. Locked in some strange kind of metal suit that made the slightest movement next to impossible.

Dear God, where am I? How did I get here?

Again the sound of the voices grew and for a moment they frightened Charlie. Then the words began to make sense. This wasn't the hissing of invisible demons. It was singing. Something familiar and wonderful and filled with joy.

The song built and grew and became the song Charlie loved best at Christmastime. "O Holy Night."

Father, am I with You in heaven? Am I dreaming?

He remembered the van sliding out of control . . . the sounds of breaking glass and wrenching metal and . . . He had been in a terrible accident. That's what had happened. But then why was everyone around him singing? The answer dawned on him gradually. He had to be in heaven. What other reason could there be?

If he were in heaven, then he hadn't had the chance to tell Donna good-bye. He wouldn't see her again— maybe for decades—and despite the joyful singing and the laughter that followed, the thought made Charlie sadder than he'd been in all his life. In all of heaven, he wanted only one thing.

The feel of Donna's arms around him.

Then the strangest thing happened. Charlie felt a tear slide down his cheek, and suddenly nothing made sense. There was no crying in heaven. The Bible taught him that. If he wasn't in heaven, he had to be . . .

He had to be alive!

Donna . . . I'm here.

"Charlie, it's me, honey. It's Donna."

She was standing right beside him. He felt the touch of her fingers against his face.

Like the rising sun, light began to fill his senses. He wasn't sure how long it took—whether an hour or five minutes passed—but with Donna's voice encouraging him, he opened his eyes. Just a crack at first. The light was blinding, and someone must have realized it, because the light dimmed again and he could open his eyes a little more.

Things were blurry, his mind fuzzy. He wasn't dead. That much was clear. A man who looked like a doctor came up beside him and raised the back of his bed. Only a few inches, but the higher position allowed him to see objects, dark blurs, and lighter smeary areas. He blinked again and again.

"Charlie. I'm here."

Donna! Charlie wasn't sure how much time was passing. The process felt slow and fast and amazing all at the same time. More blinking, and as if the fog had lifted, he could see. Not just colors and shapes but people.

He shifted his eyes and winced at the pain it caused him, and there she was. His sweet Donna. He blinked once more, and she came clearer into view. He couldn't talk. The doctor was saying something. He was waking up . . . good signs . . . vitals good. Charlie realized that something was in his throat. Sticking out of his throat. He reached up to grab it but couldn't lift his hand. Not all the way.

"Hold on there, Charlie." The doctor leaned over the bed and stared straight at him. "You're waking up quickly, and that's a good thing. Give me a minute to see how you're breathing."

Charlie forced himself to relax, to look at the faces of the people gathered around him. Why had they all come? How had they known? It hit him exactly who he was looking at. These weren't just any people. They were customers.

His family.

Around the room, Donna watched several of Charlie's friends start to cry. It was one thing to pray for a Christmas miracle, to believe in one. It was something else entirely to see it happen before their eyes. Charlie moved again and again, twitching and shifting beneath the sheets. He was coming back to Donna, but in what condition? Would he know her? Would he remember The Bridge and the people who loved him? Before she could let her fears consume her, she saw something else.

A tear rolling down Charlie's cheek.

That single tear told Donna that the tenderhearted Charlie she had spent a lifetime loving was in there. As the doctor joined them in the room and smiled at the monitors, as the miracle continued to play out, Donna was filled with heavenly peace and one consuming thought.

This was a holy night she would remember as long as she lived.

CHAPTER ELEVEN

Molly had never seen a miracle before.

She never knew until now that they were really something that happened. Like everyone in the room, she watched the scene through a veil of tears, unable to believe that here—on Christmas Eve—Charlie Barton was waking up.

The doctor explained to the group that Charlie needed a quieter room for the waking-up process. "It's happening very fast. That's a good sign." He checked the clock. "I'd like to monitor him for the next several hours. If you could come back . . . maybe after dinner?"

Molly pulled Ryan aside as they headed for the elevator. "I have some business to take care of. I'll meet you for dinner before we head back here."

"Okay." He looked surprised and a little hurt. They

made a plan to meet at a diner on Main Street in downtown Franklin. Molly called for a ride and spent the next few hours in the office of a branch of her bank. She finished what she'd set out to do ten minutes before the bank's early closing.

Others from the group joined them for dinner, so the conversation wasn't focused on the two of them. Molly was grateful. This trip was about Charlie and The Bridge and maybe finding a faith that had never mattered much. A second chance for Charlie and for her. It was most definitely not about recapturing some long-lost connection with Ryan Kelly. Never mind that they were both single. Ryan wasn't interested, no matter what Molly once thought she'd seen in his eyes.

The truth hurt. The sooner she could get home, the better.

———

They gathered in the lobby, and Molly listened with the others while Ryan placed the call to Donna. "We're here. Can we come up?"

Whatever the answer, Ryan's eyes shone with fresh hope. He assured Donna they'd be there in a few minutes. Then he hung up and looked at the fifteen or so who had gathered. Many of them had returned for this visit, and all of them waited in silence for Ryan's report.

"He's awake. Breathing on his own." His voice caught and he stopped for a moment. He pinched the bridge of his nose and gave a shake of his head, trying to find his voice. He coughed a few times and tried again. "Sorry. It's just . . . he knows who he is. The doctor said he has some confusion, but he doesn't appear to have any permanent damage."

Molly's knees felt week. No damage? After suffering a head injury and lying in a coma for nearly two weeks? *Maybe, God, You really did hear our prayers.*

The others started talking among themselves, remarking that a recovery like this was hardly possible. Let alone on Christmas Eve. Ryan raised his hand to get their attention once more. Molly hated herself for thinking it, but he had never looked more handsome. "Listen up." He looked more serious. "Donna will take the lead. Charlie doesn't know about the books or any of it. He has only mentioned The Bridge once—when Donna asked if he knew where he worked."

A ray of light shone in Molly's soul. She could hardly wait to get to the sixth floor.

It took both elevators to get the group to the sixth floor, and this time they walked into the room quietly, respectful of any confusion their arrival might cause. They filled in the empty spaces of the room, and Molly took the spot beside Donna. Ryan looked for her as he entered at the back of the group. She turned away, and he found a place at the foot of Charlie's bed.

Charlie was sitting almost completely up. The tube in his throat was removed, and as he looked at the faces around him, he reached for Donna's hand.

"They came, Charlie." She leaned in close to him. "Because of The Bridge, they came."

A few of their names came across his lips but he was difficult to understand. His voice was raspy, the result of the respirator. Donna nodded at Ryan, and he stepped forward. "Hi, Charlie." His eyes were damp, his smile shining from deep in his soul. "Merry Christmas."

Charlie squinted a little, as if he couldn't believe what he was seeing. "Ryan Kelly."

"Yes." Ryan smiled and pointed to the others around him. "We all stopped by to give you a gift."

Charlie raised his eyebrows, the look in his eyes as sweet as before the flood. "A gift?"

"Yes, Charlie." Donna took hold of his hand. "Look over there."

For what must have been the first time since he woke up, Charlie shifted his attention to the side of the room. Ryan walked to the first box and picked up a book at the top of the pile. "Books. We all pulled together a few boxes of books. So you can still be a bookseller, Charlie."

"Books?" The raspy whisper couldn't hide the shock. He turned slowly to Donna and then back to Ryan. "Every box?"

"Enough books to fill your store." Ryan walked back to the foot of the bed. He gave Charlie's foot a tender squeeze. "It's the least we can do. After all you've done for us."

Molly felt like she was watching a scene from a movie. In bits and spurts, the news seemed to sink in, and Charlie Barton began to cry. Not in a loud or desperate sort of way, the tears of a man whose struggle had taught him something.

He was not alone.

"That's not all." Donna took over. She faced him

and put her hand alongside his face. "People have given money, Charlie. So you can buy whatever books you don't have in those boxes."

His smile lit up the room, and his tears slowed. Just as quickly, his expression fell, and he looked at Donna. He didn't say anything, but Molly could imagine what he was thinking. What good were books without a store? Before anyone could say anything, a nurse worked her way through the crowd. She was holding a large manila envelope over her head. "Donna Barton."

"Yes?" Donna turned and faced the woman.

"This was left at the front desk for you. It's marked urgent."

Molly took a few steps back and leaned against the wall. Though she had a flight to catch in a few hours, she would've missed it to watch the next few minutes.

The others looked on, curious, while Donna opened the envelope and pulled out a few pieces of paper. As she began to read, her face grew pale and she dropped slowly to the chair. She lifted one trembling hand and put it on her husband's shoulders. "I . . . don't believe it."

"What?" Charlie spoke a little louder than before.

His energy seemed to be returning at a rapid rate. "Read it."

Donna looked at the people gathered around her but paid no special attention when she glanced at Molly.

This is good, Molly smiled to herself. No one needed to ever know. No one but Ryan. And she would be gone before he could ask about it. She moved a few steps closer to the door, her eyes on Donna.

"The first piece of paper is from the bank. Confirming that an anonymous source has purchased the building that housed The Bridge."

A chorus of quiet gasps and whispered discouragement rose from the room. Ryan took a step closer. "Charlie still has a week. It's not the first of the year yet."

"Wait." Donna smiled, but the shock in her lined features remained. She held up the second piece of paper. "This explains everything. It's a letter." She looked at Charlie. "From one of your customers." She took a slow breath. "It says: 'Dear Charlie, it came to my attention that you and The Bridge had fallen on hard times. I have to believe you'll be awake to hear this. The truth is, I couldn't stand by and watch your bookstore fail. The years I spent at The Bridge were the best in all my life. So I bought the building, Charlie.'"

Concern held expressions motionless. The room remained utterly quiet but for the sound of Donna's voice as she continued to read. "'Once, a long time ago, I watched you sell a book to a single mother for a penny. From now on and as long as you wish to run The Bridge, that shall be your annual lease. One cent. The truth is, I would do anything for you, sir. Anything that was right.'"

Silent tears fell on the faces of Charlie's friends, but Molly barely noticed. She was looking at Ryan, and of course, he was looking at her. The line from *Jane Eyre* was proof positive of where the gift had come from. She smiled at him for what would be the last time. Then she turned to Charlie and Donna, who was crying and laughing and hugging Charlie. "You don't have to close, Charlie. Once you're better, you can open The Bridge."

There were no tears on Charlie's face, not this time. Instead he was smiling, looking toward the window, his eyes shining with an innocence and awe usually reserved for children and angels. As if he knew better than to look for an explanation among the people in the room.

Not when the only answer was God alone.

Molly stepped into the hall and remembered something. Her copy of *Jane Eyre*. She had to get to the airport if she didn't want to miss her flight. But maybe she had enough time. Besides, some things were more important than being home for Christmas. She headed for the elevator, and as the door closed behind her, she smiled. Her prayers had been heard. Maybe not for her and Ryan. But for Charlie Barton. Which meant God was exactly who the pastor had claimed He was.

The God of second chances.

CHAPTER TWELVE

She wasn't coming back.

Ryan knew because of the look on her face. The sense of finality and good-bye mixed with a raw pain deeper than anything Ryan had seen in her. As soon as she stepped out of the room, he knew. She was gone. He watched her leave, watched her turn away and disappear, and there was nothing he could do, no way to stop her. Not without upsetting Charlie.

He hurried the remainder of the visit as best he could, and ten minutes later, when everyone was saying good-bye, Donna came up to him. "Ryan, how can we ever thank you?"

"One way." He hugged her. "Reopen The Bridge." He glanced at the clock on the wall. Molly had been gone eleven minutes. He didn't want to rush the moment, but he needed to go. Needed to find her before she boarded the plane. If he let her get away now, he might not have another chance.

Ryan looked back at Charlie. He was visiting with the others. "Donna, I need to run. Tell Charlie I'll be back tomorrow."

"I will." The creases in her forehead deepened. "Wait—where's Molly? I didn't see her go."

"She had to catch a plane." He frowned. "I think she was running late."

"Tell her about the lease. I bet she missed it." Joy and hope and life danced in the older woman's eyes. "Molly should know what happened. It's a miracle."

"Yes. I'll be sure to tell her." Ryan took a few steps toward the door. "See you tomorrow."

He rushed to the elevator, and once he was out the door of the hospital, he flew to his truck, his pounding feet keeping time with his heart. *God, please . . . where would she go? Don't let her get away yet. I know she's married, but this might be my last chance to talk to her. Please.*

Only when he was halfway out of the parking lot did he see the piece of paper. There, tucked beneath his windshield wipers, was something that looked like a note. He slammed on his brakes, jumped out of the truck, and grabbed it. The sky was clear, so the paper wasn't wet. He held it up to the parking lot light and read it.

Ryan, it was nice seeing you. Good luck with the next tour. Molly.

What was this? Anger coursed through him. He crushed the piece of paper in his fist, and threw it to the floorboards. That was all? A quick "good luck" and she was gone? So she was married. Did that mean she couldn't give him a proper good-bye when they'd probably never see each other again?

She couldn't leave like this.

He squealed out of the parking lot and headed to the airport, driving like a maniac until the light ahead turned red. "Come on!" The Nashville airport was at least twenty minutes away. He stared at the signal and checked for cross-traffic. No one was coming. For a serious moment he thought about running it. At the same time, a voice of reason shouted to be heard. *What are you doing? Chasing after her? Driving to the airport and then what?* He would have to park and guess at her airline. By the time he got it right, she'd be through security, and it would be too late.

Same as it always was with Molly.

The unexplainable thing was that she wanted him to know. The reference to *Jane Eyre* in the letter left him no doubt who the mysterious donor was. She was waiting for him to look at her as Donna read the last lines of the letter. For what? So he'd know she had a heart? He already knew that. She'd given it to some other guy before Ryan had a chance. The light turned green, but he felt the fight leave him. Forget the airport. He wouldn't find her, anyway. Instead he would go to The Bridge. He had one more book to give, the one on the seat beside him.

His copy of the Brontë novel.

He hadn't planned to give it away, but after seeing Molly's wedding ring, he'd changed his mind. She had long since moved on. What good would it do to keep something that stirred so many emotions in him, so many memories? Seeing her these past few days had confirmed what he'd always denied in himself: In the deepest part of his heart, he had always held out hope. If he kept the book, if he remembered the girl who gave it to him, then maybe someday they'd find each other again. She'd come back and she'd be single and they could figure out what went wrong.

Now that hope was dead, so his copy of the book would be the first in Charlie Barton's new collection.

He settled into his seat and turned his truck south toward Franklin.

———

Main Street was pitch dark. Besides the half-moon, only the occasional dim light from inside a closed storefront provided any light at all. Ryan didn't care. He parked his truck in front of The Bridge, climbed out, and leaned against his hood. Charlie Barton was awake and had his store back. What more could Ryan ask for? Especially when everything about the last few days with Molly felt like nothing more than a dream.

He was about to get the key and walk inside when he noticed something. The front door was open a few inches. Franklin didn't have a large community of homeless people, but that had to be it. Someone without electricity and a roof over his head had found a way inside. Ryan wanted to be careful.

Moving without a sound, he came to the front door and listened. A shuffling noise echoed through the empty storefront. The movement seemed to come from upstairs. Ryan took a deep breath and crept inside. If someone were sleeping here, that was one thing; especially with the store in this condition. But if vandals were having their way with the place, he'd have to take action.

He was about to move past the front counter when he heard another sound. A voice or maybe a video player. He couldn't make it out, exactly. Adrenaline poured into his veins and put him on edge. What were these noises? Not until he reached the stairs did he realize what he was hearing.

Someone was crying. Sobbing. Soft and muffled and hopeless. His concern doubled. Whatever the situation, it no longer felt dangerous. He moved catlike up the stairs and peered around the corner, and what he saw made him nearly call her name out loud. It was her, of course. Even from the back he recognized her immediately, her blond hair catching the light of the moon from the nearby window. Molly Allen wasn't on a flight back to Portland.

She was here.

Sitting cross-legged on the floor in the exact spot where they had spent so many afternoons, her face in her hands, her heart clearly breaking. She hadn't heard him until now, but something must have caught her attention, because she shifted and sat up straighter, glancing over her shoulder into the dark room.

He didn't want to scare her. So he did what he would've done seven years ago if he'd known he wasn't going to see her again. He didn't need the book. The lines were in his heart. "'I am no bird; and no net ensnares me.'" He hesitated. "What happened to that girl?"

"Ryan!" She allowed a quick gasp and spun around, facing him. "What are you doing here?"

He came closer and sat on the floor opposite her, their knees inches apart. "That was supposed to be my question."

The shock looked to be wearing off, but she seemed discouraged, resigned in some way he couldn't quite understand. "You . . . you're supposed to be at the hospital."

"And you're supposed to be at the airport."

"I missed my flight." She exhaled, finding control again. But something in her tone was more hurt than defeated. "What did that mean? The *Jane Eyre* quote?"

"What happened to her?" He shrugged. "You didn't give me a chance to ask."

Molly dried her eyes with the sleeves of her sweater and looked at him. She couldn't maintain the connection now any more than she could earlier that day. She let her eyes find a spot on the wooden floor. "I play violin for a local symphony." Her tone settled a bit more. She lifted her eyes to his again. "No net ensnares me, Ryan. I'm still that girl."

She played the violin? He forced himself to remember that they weren't sophomores in college, and this wasn't the backyard of her parents' home. He could barely concentrate outside of the way he was drawn to her. "You didn't tell me. About the violin."

Her face didn't apologize. "You didn't ask." She angled her head, allowing him to see a little deeper into her soul. "When we first met, you told me you might have questions. I told you I might have answers, remember that?"

"Yes." He slid back a little, fighting his emotions. "I remember everything."

"This time you didn't ask." She lifted her chin a little. "You don't know anything about me, Ryan Kelly."

She was right. That was the worst part. He sighed, wishing he could explain himself. He hadn't felt right asking questions, not when she had a man waiting back at home. "Okay." He leaned forward, his elbows on his knees. "Your husband . . . does he like music?" His voice was soft, the question merely his attempt at a window to her heart. The one he hadn't looked for earlier. "And does he know about your obsession with *Jane Eyre*?"

Her gaze fell. For a long time she said nothing, only stared at the floor again and moved her fingers nervously along the old wooden planks. Finally, a shaky breath slid across her lips, and two fresh tears fell onto her cheeks. When she looked up, her eyes were the same as they'd been back at the hospital. Filled with a raw pain that made no sense. "Ryan."

It took all his strength to keep from drawing her close and finding a way to comfort her. "Talk to me, Molly."

Before the words would come, the look in her eyes changed. As if, whatever she was about to say, she was already begging him to understand.

"Look, I never stopped caring about you, Molly. I hate seeing you like this." He reminded himself to be careful, not to say too much. "You and your husband . . . is there a problem?"

She pressed her fist to her forehead, and when she lowered it, she said the words he never expected. "I'm not married." She twisted the ring on her left hand. "This is my mother's wedding band."

Ryan heard the words; he just couldn't register them. Couldn't find a place where they made even a little sense. She wasn't married? The ring wasn't hers? He closed his eyes and then blinked them open. He didn't move, couldn't breathe. The assault of emotions on his heart was so varied, he had no idea which one to tackle first.

Shock seemed to take the lead. "Why, Molly?"

Her voice fell to a whisper, tears choking her words. "It was safer."

"But . . ." His own eyes were damp now. "You hate safe. Remember?"

"Except with you."

Ryan remembered her father's phone call. None of it made sense, why Molly would have run to the guy if she hadn't been in love with him. "All this time I thought you married him." He stood and paced to the window. When he turned around, shock took a backseat to anger. "Why did you call him if you weren't in love with him?"

"What?" She sounded mystified.

"The night we kissed, you called *him*, not me." He didn't hide his fury. For seven years he'd wanted to have this conversation with her. He found a level of restraint. "Don't act surprised. Your father told me." He could feel the disgust in his expression. "He even played me the message."

With that, her eyes no longer held an apology or a broken heart or righteous indignation. They held sheer and complete horror. In that single moment he knew with absolute certainty that he'd based the last seven years on nothing more than a lie.

A wicked, ruinous, heartless lie.

CHAPTER THIRTEEN

Molly tried to get up, tried to scream out over the news, but she could do neither. Instead she rose to her knees and leveled her gaze straight at him, at all he knew about the past that she hadn't known until now. When she could catch her breath, she said only the necessary words. "Tell me everything."

Ryan looked like he'd been shot through the heart, as if the life he'd believed in for almost a decade was emptying onto the floor around him. "You didn't call Preston that night?"

"After we kissed?" She heard the pain in her voice. Even from the grave, her father had manipulated her life. "Really, Ryan? Did you actually believe that?"

He came to her and held out his hands. "This is going to hurt us both." He helped her to her feet. "I won't have this conversation without you close to me."

The feel of his fingers against hers weakened her defenses, and she knew he was right. Whatever was coming next, she wanted nothing more than to hear it from the safety of his arms. His fingers eased between hers, and she felt her head spin. She wanted details, answers, but not as much as she wanted him. She closed her eyes and tried to assess the damage her father had wreaked on her life.

It was too great to get her mind around.

He drew a slow breath. "The staff must've told your dad about our kiss."

"Nice."

"However he found out, the next morning he called me."

"How?" She started to pull away, but he wouldn't let her. "He called on your cell?"

"Yes. He told me not to worry about how he got my number."

She groaned and hung her head. How could her dad have done this? "He had a friend on the board at Belmont." She wanted to run, hide her face from Ryan for all her father had put them through. "What did he say?"

"He basically forbade me to have feelings for you."

Ryan's words were slower, kinder. As if he were well aware of the pain they were causing her. "He told me a boy from Carthage, Mississippi, would never be good enough for you."

"What?" The word was more of a cry. "That was never true."

Ryan didn't stop. "He also told me that you were engaged to Preston Millington. He told me you'd set a date and that you had called Preston the night before—after being with me."

Molly felt faint, felt herself losing hearing and vision and consciousness. "No . . . he couldn't have done that." She tried again to take a step back; this time he eased his arms around her waist.

"I'm sorry . . . I know this is hard." He whispered the words against her face. "I'm not letting you go this time."

She pressed her head against his chest and wished with all her being that when she opened her eyes, it would be seven years earlier and they would've had this conversation before she left. "You said . . . something about a message." She eased back enough to see his face.

"Yes. He played me a message." This part was hard

for Ryan; that much was obvious. Clearly, he had based his belief in her father's words entirely on what had happened at the end of the phone call. "It was your voice." He sighed, deeply discouraged. "I'd like to say I've forgotten what you said, but I haven't. I heard you say, 'Yes, Preston . . . you know how I feel about you. I've known you all my life. You always knew I wouldn't stay at Belmont forever.'"

The light-headed feeling was back, and the room began to spin. The words were familiar, and if Ryan said they were her voice, then they must've been. When had she said that? Her senior year, maybe? Or the summer before she left for college? As she forced her brain to go back, the picture came into focus.

Preston had called from her father's office the day before she moved to Nashville. The entire conversation felt like nothing more than a plea on his part, his way of begging her to forget her plans for Belmont. So she had reassured him. After all the years of boarding school, he had to have known how she felt about him. Like he was her friend. Nothing more. That was what she had meant. She explained to Ryan despite the sick feeling trying to consume her.

When she was finished, the next realization almost

leveled her. "My father . . . he was in the room." The admission was sickening. "He records calls on his business line. So he must've saved my side of the conversation. He probably planned on using it to convince me how I felt." She raked her hand through her hair, sick to her stomach. "My dad knew I didn't love Preston. He tried everything he could to convince me I did."

The story made sense to Ryan. She could see that much in his face. "Or in case he ever needed to use the recording to keep a boy from Carthage away from his only daughter." His obvious disbelief dropped his voice to a whisper. "I can't believe this."

"Exactly." Molly wouldn't blame him if he hated her for the way her father had treated him. "I can't believe he'd lie to you." She looked deep into Ryan's eyes, all the way through him. "Can I tell you something?"

"Please." He ran his thumbs along her hands, his eyes locked on hers.

"I never would've called anyone that night." Her eyes locked on his. "All I could think about was you. That night . . . it was one of the best in my life."

He stared at her, defeated once again. She watched a pair of tears slide down his cheeks. "Then why, Molly? Why'd you leave?"

"Because." She shrugged one shoulder, her lip quivering. "You didn't want me. You apologized the next day. And an apology after a night like that was as good as telling me you never wanted to kiss me again."

"Molly." He released the hold he had on her waist and ran his fingers down the length of her arms. "I missed you every day since then. I thought you were married, but still"—he pulled his copy of *Jane Eyre* from his pocket—"I kept this. Hoping that maybe someday I'd see you again." Another bit of understanding filled his expression. "Everything had changed . . . you wrote that at the back of my book. Because of my apology?"

"I did." She managed a weak smile despite the tears in her eyes. "It's why I wore the ring." Her heart felt like it had been in knots for seven years and only now was it finally beginning to unravel. "I didn't want your pity. Not if you were sorry for kissing me."

He looked like he had a hundred things he might say. Instead he did the one thing she was desperate for him to do. Slowly, with the buildup of far too long, he pulled her to himself and kissed her, a kiss that erased seven years in as many seconds. His lips against hers, the feel of his strong arms around her shoulders. All of it was like some wonderful dream, as if the Ryan in the video had stepped into her world.

All she wanted was to never wake up.

———————

Molly didn't look away, wouldn't dare take her eyes off him, because if she did, he might not be there when she looked back.

"You should know something." His eyes danced.

Molly understood how he could look so happy. With the lies cleared up, there was no distance between them. No lies or doubts or hurt feelings. "What should I know?"

He linked his arms around her waist once more and swayed with her gently, dancing to the sound of creaking boards in their favorite room at The Bridge. "You should know that I've always wanted to kiss you." His grin continued to lighten the mood between them. "Even when I thought you were married."

"Ryan!" She giggled, and then the reality of what he'd said sank in. "You've always wanted to kiss me?"

"Always. From the first day I saw you in the auditorium during orientation."

"Why didn't you say anything?" Her voice fell to a whisper. She put her hand on his cheek, searching his eyes. "We lost so much time."

"Not anymore."

"So what do we do?" Her mind spun with the impossibilities of their lives, the logistics they would need to work out. "My office is in Portland."

"You mean your Portland office is in Portland." He swayed with her again, his eyes sparkling in the soft light from the window. "Your Nashville office will be here. Isn't that what you meant?"

He made it sound so easy, but after a few seconds of wrestling with herself, she realized he was right. With her money, she could open branches in ten cities. "So I move to Nashville?"

"Tomorrow." He kissed her again and one more time. When he drew back, he spoke straight to her soul. "You marry me, and I chase my dream of being a studio musician, and when the babies come . . . you know where we'll take them, right?"

She laughed, not believing this was real, that he was actually saying these things. Marriage? And babies? The joy in her heart was as foreign as it was wonderful. "Where do we take them?"

"To The Bridge, of course."

"Right. Because someone has to teach our little girl that no net will ever ensnare her."

"Mmm." He kissed her again.

She let herself get lost in the feeling. When she took a breath, she whispered near his face. "Is this happening? Are we really doing this?"

"Dreams don't feel this good." His voice was thick with passion. When he kissed her the next time, he seemed to force himself to take a step back. "Don't leave me, Molly. Ever again."

She smiled. "I kept your memory alive. Every year on the same day."

"You did?" They were completely comfortable together. As if no time had passed between them. "When?"

"Black Friday."

"Nice. A reference to your hatred for me, I assume."

"No." She laughed. "Just wound up that way. The one day when I blocked off time after work. That's when I would play the video."

"What video?"

"Come on, Ryan." Her heart hadn't felt this good since that night in her Brentwood backyard. "The one you made for your cinematography class."

"Where I interviewed you in the car?" He chuckled at the way he'd made the project seem like a serious work of art. "You still have that?"

Her laughter faded, and her eyes held his. "I do . . . I play it every year, the day after Thanksgiving. Makes me remember how thankful I was to have you." Her smile felt sad again. "Even for only two years."

"Molly, I had no idea." He looked like he might kiss her again. Then he made a funny face. "What was the name of that video?"

"Remember?" She held onto him, wanting the moment never to end. "You called it 'The Bridge: How a Small-Town Boy from Carthage, Mississippi, and a Highbrow Girl from Pacific Heights, California, Found Common Ground on a Daily Commute Down Franklin Road Outside Music City to The Bridge— the Best Little Bookstore in the World.'"

"Worst title ever."

"I tried to tell you that." She laughed again. "You got an A, anyway."

"Here's a better title." He ran his thumb along her

cheekbone, lost in her eyes. "'Two Years and Forever . . . How a Bookstore Changed Everything.'"

"Hmmm." The longer they stayed like this, the more real it felt. The more she could practically see their life ahead the way Ryan had laid it out a few minutes ago. "I like it."

"You know something? I might want to get married right here in this room. Where it all began." Ryan kissed her one last time and then, against the demands of their desires, led her downstairs. "Let's get you back to your hotel. We both need a good night's sleep." He winked at her. "Tomorrow is Christmas."

In the craziness of the last hour, Molly had almost forgotten. She slipped into Ryan's arms, and as they reached his truck, she thought of something. "A pastor once told me that God was the giver of second chances."

"He is." Ryan's eyes made her wonder how she could've ever doubted his feelings. "I've prayed for this moment since we said good-bye. Provided you weren't married, of course."

She laughed. "As if I would marry Preston Millington. Please."

The wind had picked up, and the chill in the air

was biting cold. He swept her into his arms and held her for another long moment. Then they climbed in his truck and headed north on Franklin Road. As if her father had never lied to Ryan and his apology had never happened and she'd never gotten on a plane and left for good. Along the way, they talked and laughed and dreamed about possibilities that were suddenly real.

And as they drove, as Molly felt the warmth of her hand in his, she did the only thing left to do. Treasure the miracle.

And thank the God of second chances.

ACKNOWLEDGMENTS

No book comes together without a great and talented team of people. For that reason, a special thanks to my friends at Howard Books, who combined efforts with a number of people passionate enough about Life-Changing Fiction™ to make *The Bridge* all it could be. A special thanks to my amazing editor, Becky Nesbitt, and to Jonathan Merkh. Thanks also to the creative staff and the sales force at Howard and Simon & Schuster who worked tirelessly to put this book in your hands.

A special thanks to my amazing agent, Rick Christian, president of Alive Communications. Rick, you've always believed in only the best for me. When we talk about the highest possible goals, you see them as doable, reachable. You are a brilliant manager of my career, an incredible agent, and I thank God for you.

But even with all you do for my ministry of writing, I am doubly grateful for your encouragement and prayers. Every time I finish a book, you send me a letter worth framing, and when something big happens, yours is the first call I receive. Thank you for that. The fact that you and Debbie are praying for me and my family keeps me confident every morning that God will continue to breathe life into the stories in my heart. Thank you for being so much more than a brilliant agent.

Thanks to my husband, who puts up with me on deadlines and doesn't mind driving through Taco Bell after a football game if I've been editing all day. This wild ride wouldn't be possible without you, Donald. Your love keeps me writing; your prayers keep me believing that God has a plan in this ministry of Life-Changing Fiction™. And thanks for the hours you put in helping me. It's a full-time job, and I am grateful for your concern for my reader friends. Of course, thanks to my daughter and sons, who pull together— bringing me iced green tea and understanding my sometimes crazy schedule. I love that you know you're still first, before any deadline.

Thank you to my mom, Anne Kingsbury, and to

my sisters, Tricia and Sue. Mom, you are amazing as my assistant—working day and night sorting through the mail from my readers. I appreciate you more than you'll ever know. Traveling together these past years for Extraordinary Women and Women of Joy events has given us times that we will always treasure. Now we will be at Women of Faith events as well. The journey gets more exciting all the time!

Tricia, you are the best executive assistant I could ever hope to have. I appreciate your loyalty and honesty, the way you include me in every decision and the daily exciting website changes. My site has been a different place since you stepped in, and the hits have grown a hundredfold. Along the way, the readers have so much more to help them in their faith, so much more than a story. Please know that I pray for God's blessings on you always, for your dedication to helping me in this season of writing, and for your wonderful son, Andrew. And aren't we having such a good time? God works all things for good!

Sue, I believe you should have been a counselor! At your home far from mine, you get batches of reader letters every day, and you diligently answer them using God's wisdom and His Word. When readers get a response from "Karen's sister Susan," I hope they know how carefully you've prayed for them and the responses you give them. Thank you for truly loving what you do, Sue. You're gifted with people, and I'm blessed to have you aboard.

And to my friends at Premier (Roy Morgan and team), along with my friends at Women of Faith, Extraordinary Women, and Women of Joy, how wonderful to be a part of what God is doing through you. Thank you for including me in your family on the road.

Thanks to my forever friends and family, the ones who have been there and continue to be there. Your love has been a tangible source of comfort, pulling us through the tough times and making us know how very blessed we are to have you in our lives.

The greatest thanks to God. You put a story in my heart and have a million other hearts in mind—something I could never do. I'm grateful to be a small part of Your plan! The gift is Yours. I pray I might use it for years to come in a way that will bring You honor and glory.

It's never too late for those
willing to take a chance.

Check out the next novel coming
from Karen Kingsbury!

the CHANCE

Available March 2013

Read an excerpt in the following pages.

CHAPTER ONE

====

Summer 2002

Her mom didn't come home for dinner—third time that week.

That was the first hint Ellie Tucker had that maybe her father was right. Maybe her mother had done something so terrible that this time their family would break in two. And no one and nothing would ever put them back together again.

Ellie was fifteen that hot, humid, Savannah summer, and as the Friday afternoon hours slipped away, as six o'clock came and six-thirty went, she joined her dad in the kitchen and helped him make dinner. Tuna sandwiches with a new jar of warm mayonnaise from the cupboard. He stayed quiet, every minute of her mother's absence weighing heavy in the silence. Their refrigerator didn't have much, but he pulled out a bag of baby carrots and poured them into a bowl. With the food on the table, her dad took his spot at the head and she sat next to him.

The place across from her, the spot where her mother usually sat, remained glaringly empty.

"Let's pray." Her father took her hand. He waited for several beats before starting. "Lord, thank you for our food and our blessings." He hesitated. "You know all things. Reveal the truth, please. In Jesus's name, amen."

The truth? Ellie could barely swallow the dry bites of her sandwich. The truth about what? Her mother? The reason she wasn't home when the doctor's office where she worked closed an hour ago?

They said nothing while they ate, though the quiet screamed across the dinner table. When they were finished, her dad looked at her. His eyes were sad. "Ellie, if you would do the dishes, please." He stood and kissed her on the forehead. "I'll be in my room."

She was finishing up in the kitchen when her mom slipped through the front door. Lately Ellie felt more like the mother, or at least the way a mother was supposed to feel when their kids were teenagers. Ellie looked over her shoulder, and her eyes met her mom's. She was still wearing her black pants and white shirt, the clothes she wore for work.

"Where's your father?" Her eyes were red and swollen, her voice thick.

"In his room." She wanted to ask her mom where she'd been and why she was late. But she didn't know how. She turned back to the sink.

Ellie's mother started in that direction, then she stopped and turned to Ellie again. "I'm sorry." Her shoulders dropped a little more. "For missing dinner." She sounded weary. "I'm sorry."

Before Ellie could say anything, her mom turned and walked down the hall. Ellie checked the clock on the microwave. Seven-thirty. Her friend Nolan had another hour in the gym, another hour shooting baskets. Then Ellie would ride her bike to his house, the way she did most nights. Especially this summer.

Since her parents had been fighting.

She dried her hands, walked to her room, and shut the door behind her. A little music and some time with her journal, and then Nolan would be home. She turned on the radio. Backstreet Boys filled her room, and instantly she dropped the sound a few notches. Her dad said he'd take away her radio if she listened to worldly music. Ellie figured worldly was a matter of opinion. And her opinion was that the Backstreet Boys was as close to heaven as she was going to get for now.

The first shout rattled her bedroom window.

Ellie killed the sound on the radio and jumped to her feet. As much tension as there had been between her parents lately, neither of them did much shouting. At least not this loud. Her heart pounded. Before she reached her bedroom door, another round of shouts ripped through the air, and this time she could understand what her father was saying, the names he was calling her mom.

Quietly, too afraid to breathe, Ellie crept down the hall and across the living room, closer to her parents' bedroom door. Another burst of shouts, and now she was near enough that she could hear something else. Her mother's tears.

"You'll pack your things and leave." Her father had never sounded like this before, like he was firing bullets of hatred with every word. "I will not have you pregnant with his child and . . . and living under my roof." His voice shook the walls. "I will not have it!"

Ellie anchored herself against the wall so she wouldn't drop to the floor. Her mother was pregnant? With someone else's baby? The blood began to leave her face, and her world started to spin. Colors and sounds and reality blurred and she wondered if she would pass out. *Run, Ellie . . . run fast.* She ordered herself to move, but her feet wouldn't follow the command.

Before she could figure out which way was up again, her father stepped into the doorway and glared at her, his chest heaving with each breath. "What are you doing?"

The question hung between them, and from behind her father Ellie caught a glimpse of her mom. Sitting in their bedroom chair, her head in her hands. *Get up,* Ellie wanted to scream at her. *Defend yourself! Do something!* But her mother did nothing. She said nothing.

Ellie's eyes flew to her father again, and she tried to step away, tried to exit the scene as quickly as possible, but she tripped and fell back on her hands. Her wrists hurt but she scrambled further from him, anyway. Like a crab escaping a net.

It took that long for her father's expression to soften. "Ellie. I'm sorry." He took a step toward her. "I didn't mean for . . . you weren't supposed to hear that."

And in that moment Ellie knew two things. First, the horrible thing her dad had shouted was true. And second, her life as she knew it now lay splintered around her on the worn, thin hallway carpet in a million pieces. "I . . . I have to go." The words were barely a whisper.

Her father was saying something about this being more than a girl her age could understand and that she needed to get back to her room and pray. Something like that. But all Ellie could hear was the deafening way her heart slammed around in her chest. She needed air, needed to breathe. In a move that felt desperate, she found her way to her feet and ran for the front door. She needed Nolan, and she needed him now. A minute later she was on her bicycle pedaling through the summer night.

Pedaling as fast as she could.

━━━━━

He would still be at the gym, but that was okay. Ellie loved watching Nolan play basketball. Loved it whether the place was packed with kids from Savannah High, or just the two of them and the echo of the ball hitting the shiny wood floor. With every push of her foot against the pedal Ellie tried to put the reality out of her mind. But the truth smothered her like a wet blanket. Her mother had come home late again—the way she'd been coming home late since early spring. And today . . . today she must have told her father what he had suspected all along.

She was having an affair. Not only that, but she was pregnant.

The truth churned in her stomach, suffocating her until finally she had no choice but to ditch her bike in the closest bush and give way to the nausea consuming her. One revolting wave after another, her insides convulsing until the only thing left inside her was the hurt. A hurt that would stay with her forever.

Exhausted and drained, Ellie sat on the curb, her head in her hands, and let the tears come. Until then, the horror and shock had kept her sadness at bay. But with her stomach and heart empty, she cried until she could barely breathe. Her mom didn't love her father, which meant she didn't love Ellie, either. Their family wasn't enough for her. There was no other way to look at this. A sense of shame added itself to the mix of sorrow. Nolan's mom would never have done something like this.

She lifted her face to the darkening sky. Nolan. Ellie wiped her face and breathed in deep. She needed to get to him before it got any later, needed to find him before he left the gym. She forced the pedals to move faster, willed the old bike to make time until finally the gym was in sight. The sound of the ball hitting the floor filled her ears as she leaned her bike against the brick wall at the back of the building, next to his.

Nolan kept the door propped open in case a breeze might come up. Ellie slipped through the entrance and moved quietly to the first row of the bleachers. Nolan caught the ball and stared at her, his eyes dancing, a smile tugging at his lips. "You're early."

She nodded. She didn't trust her voice, not when all she wanted to do was run to him and let him wrap his arms around her. Nolan Cook. Her best friend in the whole world.

"Ellie?" A shadow of concern fell over his handsome face. "You okay?"

As much as she wanted to go to him, she couldn't tell him. Didn't want him to know why she was upset, because then . . . well, then for sure it would be true. There would be no turning from the truth once she told Nolan.

He set the ball down and walked to her. Sweat dripped from his forehead, and his tank top and shorts were drenched. "You've been crying." He stopped a foot from her. "What happened?"

"My parents." She felt her eyes well up, felt her words drown in an ocean of sadness.

"More fighting?"

"Yeah. Bad."

"Ahh, Ellie." His breathing was returning to normal. He wiped his forearm across his face. "I'm sorry."

"Keep playing." Her voice sounded strained from her heartache. She nodded to the basket. "You have another ten minutes."

He watched her for a long couple of seconds. "You sure?"

"We can talk later. I just"—a few tears slid down her cheeks—"needed to be here. With you."

Again he studied her, but eventually he nodded. Slow and not quite sure. "Okay. We can leave whenever you want."

"When you're done. Please, Nolan."

One last look, but then he turned and jogged back to the ball. Once it was in his hands he dribbled to the left and the right, and then took the ball to the hoop. In a move as fluid and graceful as anything Ellie had seen in her seven years of dance lessons, Nolan rose in the air and slammed the ball through the net. He landed lightly on both feet and caught the ball. Dribbled back out, juked a few more imaginary opponents, and repeated the move. Ten straight dunks, and then he jogged to the drinking fountain and drank for half a minute. Next came his three-point shots.

Nolan played basketball with his heart, mind, and soul. The ball was an extension of his hand, and every move, every step was as natural for him as breathing. Watching him, Ellie felt her eyes dry, felt herself marveling at the gift he'd been given, the way she celebrated it every time she had the privilege of seeing him play. Nolan's dream was as simple as it was impossible.

He wanted to play in the NBA. It was something he prayed about and worked toward every day. Every hour of every day. From the A's and B's he struggled to earn in class to the hours he put in here every day and night. If Nolan didn't wind up playing professional basketball, it wouldn't be for lack of trying. Not for lack of believing.

He hit five shots from every spot along the arch of the three-point line, then he gulped down more water and finally tucked the ball under his arm and walked back to her. He used his shirt to wipe the sweat off his face. "Could it be more humid?"

"Yeah." She smiled a little and looked at the open back door. "Not much of a breeze."

"No." He led the way. "Come on. We'll go to my house first. I'll shower, and then we can go to the park."

That's all Ellie wanted, a few hours alone with Nolan at Gordonston Park. The place with their favorite oak tree and enough soft grass for them to lay on their backs and watch shooting stars on more summer nights than she could count. She didn't say anything, not yet. They walked silently out the back door, which Nolan closed and locked. Nolan's dad was the coach, and he had given him a key a year ago. Too much trouble to open the gym every time Nolan wanted to shoot baskets.

They rode their bikes down Pennsylvania Avenue and then took the shortcut down Kinzie Avenue to

Edgewood. Nolan's house was only half a mile from Ellie's, but they might as well have been in separate worlds for how different they were. Nolan's neighborhood had fireflies and front lawns that stretched on forever. Ellie's had chain link fences and stray dogs, with low-slung, single-story houses the size of Nolan's garage.

The sort of house Ellie and her parents lived in.

Ellie sat with Nolan's mother in the kitchen while he showered. Her eyes were dry still, so she didn't have to explain herself. Instead, the conversation was light, with Nolan's mom telling her about the new Bible study she'd joined, and how much she was learning about the Old Testament.

Ellie wanted to care, wanted to feel as connected to God as Nolan and his parents. But if God loved her, why was her life falling apart? Maybe He only loved some people. Good folks like the Cook family. A few minutes later Nolan came down in clean shorts and a T-shirt. He grabbed two chocolate chip cookies from a plate on the kitchen counter and kissed his mother's cheek.

Suddenly Nolan looked different, more grown up. She was with him every day, so she didn't always stop and notice, but here, in his kitchen, she could see it. He wasn't a kid anymore. Neither of them were. They'd been friends since second grade, and they'd walked home together since the first day of middle school. She still felt like a kid, but somewhere along the journey of time they'd both done something they hadn't seen coming.

They'd gotten older. They'd grown up.

Nolan was just over six feet already, tanned from his morning runs, his short blond hair cut close to his head the way it was every summer. He'd been lifting weights for basketball, so maybe that was why he looked different: the way his shoulders and biceps filled out the pale green T-shirt as he grabbed the cookies.

Ellie felt her cheeks grow hot and she looked away. Mrs. Cook smiled at her, and Ellie was grateful the woman hadn't caught her looking at Nolan. "Come by any time, Ellie. The door's always open. You know that."

"Yes, ma'am. Thank you." And with that they were out the door. There was no need to talk about where they were going. It was the same place every time. Beneath the biggest oak tree in the park—maybe the biggest oak tree in the city. The one dripping with Spanish moss, with the gnarled tree roots jutting out of the soft Southern ground high enough to make a place for them to sit. The grassy patch was just a few feet away, beneath a break in the branches overhead.

The place where Ellie and Nolan had come to talk about life since the summer before sixth grade. Their place. Back then they played hide-and-seek among the trees, with the enormous old oak serving as home base. During the school year, when it was warm enough, they'd do their homework out here. And on nights like this, they would do what came easiest for them.

They would simply sit down, open their hearts, and share whatever came pouring out.

"Okay. Tell me." Nolan took the spot closest to the massive tree trunk. He leaned back, studying her. "What happened?"

Ellie had been thinking about this moment since she walked through the door of the high school gym. She had to tell him the truth, because she told him everything. But she didn't have to tell him this very minute, right? He was waiting for an answer. Her throat was dry, so her words took longer to form. "My mom . . . she was late again."

He waited, and after a few seconds he blinked. Twice. "That's it?"

"Yeah." She didn't like postponing the truth, but she couldn't tell him yet. "My dad was really mad."

"Oh. I was worried it was something really bad." He leaned back against the tree. "It'll be okay, Ellie. It will."

"Right." She moved to the spot beside him and pressed her back lightly against the tree trunk. Their shoulders were touching, a reminder of everything good and right in her life.

"One day when we're old and married we'll come back to this very spot and remember tonight."

"How do you know?"

He looked at her. "That we'll remember?"

"No." She grinned. "That I'll marry you."

"That's easy." He faced her fully, shrugged, and folded his arms. "You'll never find anyone who loves you like I do."

It wasn't the first time he'd said this. And always he kept his tone light, so she couldn't accuse him of being too serious or trying to change their friendship to something more. Not yet, anyway. Always she would laugh and shake her head, as if he'd suggested something crazy like the two of them running off and joining the circus.

But this time she didn't laugh or joke or push the subject. She only lifted her eyes to the distant trees and the fireflies still dancing among them. Good thing she hadn't told him about her mother, about how she'd slept with another man and gotten pregnant. Because that would change everything. Nolan would feel sorry for her, and there would be no more teasing about marriage. Not when her parents had made such a mess of theirs.

Ellie exhaled, content. The news could wait.

Because right now she wanted nothing more than to sit here beside Nolan Cook under the big oak tree at the edge of the park on a summer night that was theirs alone and believe . . . believe for one more moment the one thing Ellie wanted more than her next breath.

That they might stay this way forever.